P9-CQK-997

CAPE HELL

Books by Loren D. Estleman

AMOS WALKER MYSTERIES

Motor City Blue
Angel Eyes
The Midnight Man
The Glass Highway
Sugartown
Every Brilliant Eye
Lady Yesterday
Downriver
Silent Thunder
Sweet Women Lie
Never Street
The Witchfinder
The Hours of the Virgin
A Smile on the Face of the Tiger
Sinister Heights
*Poison Blonde**
*Retro**
*Nicotine Kiss**
*American Detective**
*The Left-Handed Dollar**
*Infernal Angels**
*Burning Midnight**
*Don't Look for Me**
*You Know Who Killed Me**
*Sundown Speech**

VALENTINO, FILM DETECTIVE

*Frames**
*Alone**
*Alive!**
*Shoot**

DETROIT CRIME

Whiskey River
Motown
King of the Corner
Edsel
Stress
*Jitterbug**
*Thunder City**

PETER MACKLIN

Kill Zone
Roses Are Dead
Any Man's Death
*Something Borrowed, Something Black**
*Little Black Dress**

OTHER FICTION

The Oklahoma Punk
Sherlock Holmes vs. Dracula
Dr. Jekyll and Mr. Holmes
Peeper
*Gas City**
*Journey of the Dead**
*The Rocky Mountain Moving Picture Association**
*Roy & Lillie: A Love Story**
*The Confessions of Al Capone**

PAGE MURDOCK SERIES

*The High Rocks**
*Stamping Ground**
*Murdock's Law**
The Stranglers
*City of Widows**
*White Desert**
*Port Hazard**
*The Book of Murdock**
*Cape Hell**

WESTERNS

The Hider
*Aces & Eights**
The Wolfer
Mister St. John
This Old Bill
Gun Man
Bloody Season
Sudden Country
*Billy Gashade**
*The Master Executioner**
*Black Powder, White Smoke**
*The Undertaker's Wife**
*The Adventures of Johnny Vermillion**
*The Branch and the Scaffold**
*Ragtime Cowboys**
*The Long High Noon**

NONFICTION

The Wister Trace
Writing the Popular Novel

***Published by Tom Doherty Associates**

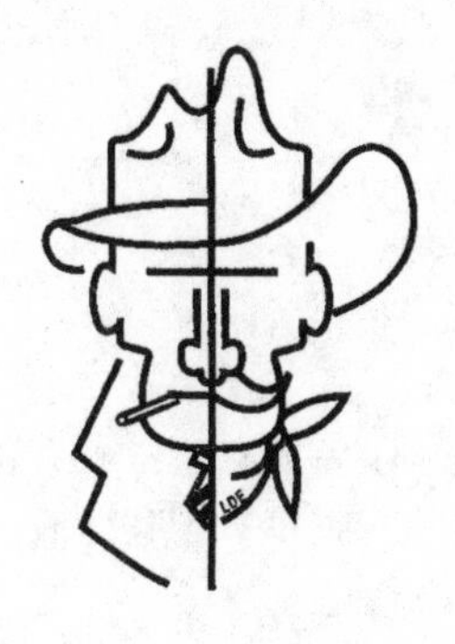

CAPE HELL

Loren D. Estleman

A TOM DOHERTY ASSOCIATES BOOK
NEW YORK

This is a work of fiction. All of the characters, organizations, and events portrayed in this novel are either products of the author's imagination or are used fictitiously.

CAPE HELL

A Forge Book
Published by Tom Doherty Associates, LLC
175 Fifth Avenue
New York, NY 10010

www.tor-forge.com

Forge® is a registered trademark of Tom Doherty Associates, LLC.

The Library of Congress Cataloging-in-Publication Data is available upon request.

ISBN 978-0-7653-8352-5 (hardcover)
ISBN 978-1-4668-9210-1 (e-book)

Our books may be purchased in bulk for promotional, educational, or business use. Please contact your local bookseller or the Macmillan Corporate and Premium Sales Department at 1-800-221-7945, extension 5442, or by e-mail at MacmillanSpecialMarkets@macmillan.com.

First Edition: May 2016

Printed in the United States of America

0 9 8 7 6 5 4 3 2 1

Robert J. Conley, in memoriam:
Heaven needed the entertainment.

"And this also," Marlow said suddenly, "has been one of the dark places of the earth."

—Joseph Conrad, *Heart of Darkness*

I

The Ghost

ONE

Halfway back to civilization, Lefty Dugan began to smell. It was my own fault, partly; I'd stopped on the north bank of the Milk River like some tenderheel fresh out of Boston instead of crossing and pitching camp on the other side. I was worn down to my ankles, and the sorry buckskin I was riding sprouted roots on the spot and refused to swim. The pack horse was game enough; either that, or it was too old to care if it was lugging a dead man or a month's worth of Arbuckle's. But it couldn't carry two, especially when one was as limp as a sack of stove-bolts and just as heavy. I was getting on myself and in no mood to argue, so I unpacked my bedroll.

A gully-washer square out of Genesis soaked my slicker clear through and swelled the river overnight. I rode three days upstream before I found a place to ford, by which time even the plucky pack horse was breathing through its mouth. In Chinook I hired a buckboard and put in to the mercantile for salt to pack the carcass, but the pirate who owned the store mistook me for Vanderbilt, and then the Swede who ran the livery refused to refund the deposit I'd made on the wagon. So I buried Lefty in the shadow of the Bearpaws and rode away from five hundred cartwheel dollars on a mount I should have shot and left to feed what the locals call Montana swallows: magpies, buzzards, and carrion crows.

The thing was, I'd liked Lefty. We'd ridden together for Ford Harper before herding cattle lost its charm, and he was always good for the latest joke from the bawdy houses in St. Louis; back then he wasn't Lefty, just plain Tom. Then he took a part-time job in the off-season blasting a tunnel through the Bitterroots for the Northern Pacific, and incidentally two fingers off his right hand.

Drunk, he was a different man. He'd had a bellyful of Old Rocking Chair when he stuck up a mail train outside Butte and was still on the same extended drunk when he drew down on me not six miles away from the spot. I aimed low, but the fool fell on his face and took the slug through the top of his skull.

Making friends has seldom worked to my advantage. They always seem to wind up on the other side of my best interests.

It was a filthy shame. Judge Blackthorne had a rule against letting his deputies claim rewards—something about keeping the body count inside respectable limits—but made an exception in some cases in return for past loyalty and present reliability, and I was one. It served me right for not allowing for Lefty's unsteady condition when I tried for his kneecap instead of his hat rack. The money was the same, vertical or horizontal.

To cut my losses, I lopped off his mutilated right hand so I could at least claim the pittance the U.S. Marshal's office paid for delivering fugitives from federal justice. I packed it in my last half-pound of bacon, making do for breakfast with a scrawny prairie hen I shot east of Sulphur Springs. I picked gristle out of my teeth for fifty miles.

The money from Washington would almost cover what I'd spent to feed that bag of hay I was using for transportation. After I sold it back to the rancher I'd bought it from just outside Helena, I was a nickel to the good. I rode the pack horse in town until it rolled over and died. I wished I'd known the beast when it was a two-year-old, and that's as much good as I've ever had to say about anything with four legs that didn't bark and fetch birds.

I spent the nickel and a lot more in Chicago Joe's Saloon, picked a fight with the faro dealer—won that one—and another with the city marshal—lost that one—and would have slept out my time in peace if the Judge himself hadn't come down personally to spring me.

"You'd better still be alive," he greeted me from the other side of the bars. "This establishment doesn't give refunds for bailing out damaged goods."

I pushed back my hat to take him in. He had on his judicial robes, but the sober official black only heightened his resemblance to Lucifer in a children's book illustration. I think he tacked the tearsheet up beside his shaving mirror so he could get the chin-whiskers just right. His dentures were in place. They'd been carved from the keyboard of a piano abandoned along the Oregon Trail, and he wore the uncomfortable things only when required by the dignity of the office. It was unlike him to go anywhere straight from session without stopping to change, especially the hoosegow. I was in for either a promotion or the sack.

"How's Ed?" I asked. The city marshal's name was Edgar Whitsunday, but only part of his first name ever made it off the door of his office. He'd been named after a dead poet, but being illiterate he sloughed off the accusation whenever it arose. He was a Pentecostal, and amused his acquaintances with his imperfect memorization of Scripture as drilled into him by a spinster aunt: I think my favorite was "I am the excrement of the Lord."

"He's two teeth short of a full house," Blackthorne said. "I told his dentist to bill Grover Cleveland."

"That's extravagant. What did you do with the rest of the piano?"

He scowled. The Judge had a sense of his own humor, but no one else's. "You realize I could declare court in session right here and find you in contempt."

"And what, put me in jail?" I looked at my swollen right hand. "At least I used my fists. Ed took the top off my head with the butt of his ten-gauge."

"You should be grateful he didn't use the other end." He sighed down to his belt buckle; it was fashioned from a medal of valor. Just what he'd done to earn it, I never knew. Even scraping forty years off his hide I couldn't picture him scaling a stockade or leading a charge up any but Capitol Hill. Probably he'd helped deliver the Democratic vote in Baltimore. "You cost me more trouble than half the men who ride for me. A wise man would let you rot."

"You make rotting sound bad." I slid my hat back down over my eyes. "Find somewhere else to distribute your largesse. This ticky cot is the closest thing I've had to a hotel bed since I rode out after Lefty."

"You can't refuse bail. Marshal Whitsunday needs this cell. The Montana Stock-Growers Association is in town, and you know as well as I those carpetbaggers will drink the place dry and shoot it to pieces."

"Good. I was getting lonesome."

"Shake a leg, Deputy. You're needed."

That made me sit up and push back my hat. He wouldn't admit needing a drink of water in the desert.

He said, "I'm short-handed. Jack Sweeney, your immediate superior, went over my head to Washington and commandeered all my best men to bring the rest of Sitting Bull's band back from Canada to face justice for Custer."

"They gave that bloody dandy justice at the Little Big Horn nine years ago. What's the rush?"

"Sweeney's contract runs out in September, and there's a Democrat in the White House." He held up a key ring the size of Tom Thumb's head and stuck one in the lock. "Go back to your hotel, clean up, and report to my chambers at six sharp."

"Since when do you adjourn before dark?"

"I swung the gavel on the Bohannen Brothers at four. You've got forty-five minutes to clean up and shave. You look like the Wild Man of Borneo and smell like a pile of uncured hides."

"How'd you convict the Bohannens without my testimony? I brought them in."

"They tried to break jail and killed the captain of the guard. That bought them fifty feet of good North Carolina hemp without your help."

"Bill Greene's dead?"

"I'm sorry. I didn't know you were close."

"He owed me ten dollars on the Fitzgerald fight. I don't guess he mentioned me in his will."

His big silver watch popped open and snapped shut. "Forty-four minutes. If I catch so much as a whiff of stallion sweat in my chambers, I'll fine you twenty-five dollars for contempt of court."

"Collect it from the stallion."

"That's twenty-five dollars you owe the United States."

I swung my feet to the floor, stood, wrestled for balance, and found it with my fists around the bars. "What's so urgent? Did we declare war on Mexico again?"

He looked as grim as ever he had during damning evidence. "What have you heard?"

TWO

When the Judge and I entered Whitsunday's office from the cells, the marshal was sitting in a captain's chair on a swivel with a pitcher of chipped ice at his elbow to ease the pain of his missing teeth. His big face behind its waxed moustaches looked like raw meat; but that was a chronic condition, having nothing to do with our recent difference of opinion.

"I'm sorry," I said, when he got up to fetch my gunbelt. "I only wanted to break your nose." It had already been twisted into so many configurations I didn't think one more would offend him; in another incarnation he'd tried his hand at prizefighting under the company name Paddy O'Reilly, and displayed with pride a rotogravure of himself in tights on the wall next to the gun rack. It had been my hard luck, when it came down to cases, to choose fists over firearms; although the butt of his shotgun had seemed too much in his favor. But then the Marquess of Queensbury couldn't pass a bank draught in the territories.

"Your aim hasn't improved since Butte, I guess," Whitsunday said.

I'd nothing to offer for that. Even in this age of telegraphy I'll never understand how news travels faster than a man on horseback; I'd thought my arrangement with Lefty Dugan less important than the cost of a wire. But a tale's a tale, which is how history gets written. I spend my leisure time reading Scripture instead. No one can argue with the Word and win.

I stopped at my hotel only long enough to grab my town clothes. At the Cathay Gardens I soaked off the sweat of two horses seasoned with forty miles of tableland and caught a shave in the King Alexander Tonsorial Parlor, making use of Minos Tetrakokis, the Judge's personal barber; charging both bills to the court, with a nickel tip. Evidently I was still employed.

The room Blackthorne used for his chambers was a stuffy varnished-oak box with a tattered Mexican flag tacked to the back wall, a large-scale map of the territory plastering the one adjacent, and the cracked and thumb-worn legal books he'd carried on his back over the Divide piled on his leather blotter. He scowled when he smelled the Parisian soap they used at the Gardens, and at the evidence of Tetrakokis' art on my pink cheeks; but he took his revenge.

"I understand they never found your bullet," he said. "It passed through his brain, down the alimentary canal, and out through the seat of his trousers, true as the Katy Flyer."

I worked the mechanism of his mahogany-paneled cabinet—a Chinese box it had taken me a year to figure out—and poured us each a tumbler of the twelve-year-old whisky he imported from San Francisco by way of Aberdeen. I handed him his and put down half my portion in a gulp. "I killed a man. A friend. He pulled me out from under a mare in the Yellowstone and pumped a half-gallon of river water out of my lungs. You came that close to losing the best deputy marshal you ever signed on."

"That would be Cocker Flynn; but point taken. I always wondered just where you developed your antipathy to our noblest beast of burden. Now I know."

"You're thinking of those civilized geldings tied up to that circus wagon you ride here in town. You can't know how it feels to be outsmarted by a creature with a pecan-size brain and a heart like stove black. That damn buckskin cheated me out of half a year's wages."

He sipped from his glass, carving deep hollows in his cheeks; the Steinway-ivory choppers were stored securely in the iron safe in the corner.

"With one breath you eulogize a friend, and with the next you complain about losing the bounty on his head. Have you any code of behavior, apart from your continued survival?"

I slid the travel-weary pocket Bible from inside my frock coat and laid my palm on the limp leather cover.

"That's your fault, your honor. You sent me to Texas in a clerical collar, purely as a pose, but it got under my skin. I had to read the book to quote from it."

He switched subjects like a yard engine.

"Are you aware of the name Oscar Childress?"

"'Women and Children' Childress?"

"An unfortunate sobriquet, possibly unearned. However, he'll most likely bear it to the grave, alongside the innocents slaughtered in Springfield, Missouri."

Legend said Childress—who'd given up a colonelship with the United States Army in order to serve as a captain under

Jefferson Davis—had stopped a trainload of civilians just outside Springfield and ordered his men to shoot them all as enemies of the Confederacy. After the war he'd led a company of volunteers into Mexico to fight alongside Juarez. This time he won. But instead of being named to high office, he'd dropped out of sight. Some said *El Presidente* himself had had him executed as a threat to his own job.

"He's resurfaced," I said then.

For the second time in an hour I'd made the old man jump. "In the Sierras," he said; "an almost impenetrable place. Once again I ask, what have you heard?"

I savored the Judge's fine whisky, knowing how bitter the chaser was bound to be. He saved the best for the men he wanted to seduce into something they'd never agree to sober.

"I've been six weeks breathing nothing but Montana topsoil," I said, "and hearing no news, short of how the wheat crop's doing. I made a joke about Mexico, which put your bowels on edge, and figured out Childress is back among the living, because you brought him up. Why bother otherwise? With respect, your honor, I'd admire to get you in a hand of poker."

He drained his glass and set it down with a thump.

"I find it interesting you should bring up the game," he said. "It's a form of war, purer than chess because of the element of chance involved."

"Not the way I play it."

"Precisely. The expedition I've in mind has no place for straight shooting and fair play. War is what I said, and war is what we're looking at if Oscar Childress and our invidious State Department has their way. He's raising an army to capture Mexico City."

"Again? That country changes hands like a Yankee dollar."

"This time he's doing it for himself. Once he has control, he intends to add the Mexican Army to his band of irregulars and rekindle the Civil War."

"Oh, that." I drank.

"Pardon me, Deputy Murdock, but am I boring you with this latest threat to the union?"

"We don't know if it's the latest until tomorrow morning. Every time I open a newspaper, someone's fixing to bring back Fort Sumter. John Wilkes Booth was seen riding a cable car in San Francisco just last week. I read about it in the barbershop."

"Some important people are taking this one seriously. I've had wires from the District, each one a brighter shade of yellow than the last. I can only assume the authorities in the border states receive them in greater frequency; however, I take it a compliment to my record that I'm included at all. No doubt there's an ambassadorship for me, in some Godforsaken country on the other side of the world, if I capture Childress."

"You mean if *I* do."

He unstopped the bell jar containing the bullet-shaped cigars he ordered from Cuba for six bits apiece and set one afire. "How's your Spanish?"

"Better than my Greek. I picked up some French on the Barbary Coast, but all that did was snarl up what little Mexican I had."

He blew a smoke ring. "You're trying to talk yourself out of an assignment."

"Without success." I finished my whisky and got up to pour myself another. It was clear I wouldn't be drinking anything but tequila for a long time.

THREE

Childress is an enigma," Blackthorne said. "Graduated West Point at the top of his class, and in the meanwhile published a slim volume of poetry that drew the attention of the eastern elite; not the helmet-headed, wing-sprouting type of epic you might expect of a warrior, but rather a deep thinker on the order of Emerson. I don't expect you to grasp the meaning of all these names."

"I read *The Conduct of Life* in a lineshack one long winter. Half of it, anyway. The hand who left it used it to start fires."

"Indeed. I can't imagine you got much out of it."

I let him have his head there. The truth was Emerson might have been writing in Chinese.

He sat back and contributed to the nicotine stain on the ceiling. "To the men who rode down there with Childress, and to not a few of the locals, he's something of a god; a man you listen to rather than discourse with, and feel yourself the better for the exchange, however you come away unenlightened by it. Before the war, there was talk of running him for the U.S. Senate.

"He's a savant, of sorts; we're just not sure what: martial, literary, political, or scientific: I'm told he submitted a treatise on galvanization to one of those boards that finds such things of interest. After Juarez's victory, he sent a letter to the U.S. State Department, recommending we exploit the peons' near-worship of our civilization to annex Mexico."

"No wonder he went underground."

"No doubt his comments led to the assumption he'd been executed. He was already under suspicion for switching his allegiance from Emperor Maximilian to the revolutionists. His success in the field spared him punishment, but once he was no longer needed—"

"That's the problem with being a born general," I said. "There isn't much call for it once peace breaks out."

"Evidently he agrees. He appears to have spent the last eighteen years assembling his own private army, comprised of former revolutionists, the remnants of his original rebel force, and the Indians who inhabit the Sierra Madre Mountains twenty miles south of the Arizona border. That's the report, in any case."

"Who wrote it?"

"A Pinkerton operative, posing as an aimless drifter. He sent a long coded wire to the agency's headquarters in Chicago and hasn't been heard from since. Numerous attempts to make contact through pre-arranged channels have failed."

"That's two Americans that country's misplaced. I didn't know it was so careless."

He picked up the bottle, frowned, then set it back down and rammed in the cork. "The obvious answer is he was found out and eliminated. Now it's up to us to confirm or disprove the report."

"Why us?"

"I volunteered the services of this court, and Washington has generously accepted."

"That was white of them. How many men did Sweeney leave us with?"

"Irrelevant. One man may succeed where a regiment would not."

"I'm supposed to comb all of Mexico looking for one Pinkerton?"

"Just the Sierras; and that isn't the mission. You're to infiltrate Childress' command and find out if there's anything to the report. If it's mistaken, or Childress is a harmless charlatan, or there's no truth to it at all, come back and report to me in person."

"And if it turns out to be right?"

"Must I express the obvious?"

"You must. It might spare me from a firing squad if I can tell the federales I killed him on your orders."

"Very well. He committed high treason the moment he offered his services to a foreign power. The penalty is death. Especially if any part of that report can be verified. The part that concerns me most is the arms he's supposed to have stockpiled: Gatlings, Napoleons, and a dozen cases of carbines. A shipment of that very number was reported missing from Winchester's warehouse in Boston. Wars have been won with less."

I uncorked the bottle and refilled my glass without asking permission.

"If I'm to start one all by myself, I'll need some things up front, starting with a decent horse."

"Black Dan Stuart is holding a bay thoroughbred for you. I made the arrangements when I heard you were back."

"A good long-distance rifle."

"Draw one from the arsenal. The deputy in charge has all the paperwork."

"Two hundred dollars in gold."

"Absolutely not. Your salary covers all your responsibilities."

"I can't bribe my way across Mexico on twenty a month."

"In lieu of receipts, I'll need a detailed record of your expenses. It will be checked."

"And a case of this Scot's courage." I lifted my glass.

"More bribery?"

"I get thirsty in the desert."

"Anything else?"

"If I think of it I'll let you know."

"Aren't you forgetting transportation?"

"You said I had a horse coming."

"You'll need it when the tracks end, but until then I'm giving you a train."

He puffed his cigar, pleased at my uncharacteristic silence.

"We don't know Childress' timetable," he said, "or even if he has one. In any case we can't risk his plans going into effect while you're crawling your way across the Sonoran Desert on horseback."

"Won't he wonder how I got my hands on a train?"

"You stole it, naturally. It's your ticket into his camp. The revolutions travel by rail down there; no self-respecting insurgent would be caught dead without one.

"Just return it when you're through playing with it," he said. "It's on loan from President Diaz, Juarez's successor. He has as much riding on this mission as we do. It's waiting for you in the railyard."

It was a smart plan. I wouldn't say it to his face. "Do I get to blow the whistle?"

"That's up to the engineer. It has a name, even if he doesn't." Blackthorne slid a fold of foolscap from an inside pocket and snapped it open. "*El Espanto.* I'm told it means 'The Ghost'; 'The Terror'; something along those lines. In some remote regions it makes sense to strike fear into the savages who'd oppose progress."

"All right," I said.

"I felt certain you'd assent eventually. I was prepared to offer to stock the saloon car with my entire cellar, had you demurred. You should have held out for more than just one case."

"I don't mind. I want to talk to Childress. He promises better conversation than I've had in a spell."

He screwed out his cigar in a heavy brass tray. "From what I've heard, he'll do all the talking."

"That's grand, too. I never learned anything listening to myself."

Which was one thing I'd said that turned out to be truer than I knew; and something I'd have torn out along with my tongue when I got the truth of it.

"Is there a settlement where I'm headed? The Sierras cover a lot of ground."

He hauled an atlas the size of a dining table from the slots where he kept his ledgers and made room to spread it on the desk.

"The map is centuries out of date. We have the pillaging Spaniards to thank for its existence at all; but nothing's come along to supplant it, and I doubt little has changed there since the death of Columbus. It's the last wild place in North America."

He ran a finger down the coast to a ragged hangnail sticking into the Gulf of California across from the mountain range.

"'Cabo Falso,'" I read.

"'The Cape of Lies.' It's home to an anonymous fishing village, the only source of communication with the outside world for a hundred miles. Even a traitor needs a conduit: That's where his alleged weaponry would have landed. If you should need to get in touch with this court, it's two weeks in the saddle from his base of operations. There's no railway spur. The only line crawls through the foothills of the Sierras; the blankest space on the map this side of darkest Africa, all craggy peaks, deep abyss, and dense jungle, teeming with mosquitoes, venomous snakes, and leeches the size of trout in Montana. I exaggerate, possibly; but better that than to underestimate the hazards. It's a pity our modern cartographers have grown too sophisticated to make allowances for dragons. If the mystical beasts were to thrive anywhere, that would be the place."

"What about women?"

"Savages, who'd mate with you and cut your throat in the moment of ecstasy; so I'm told." He flushed a little, although over the bloodshed or the carnal implication, I couldn't tell.

"I could get the same at Chicago Joe's, and save the expense of travel. Why Cape of Lies?"

Here he was on more comfortable ground.

"Legend says Cortes promised to deliver Montezuma to the natives who were rebelling against him, in return for directions to all the gold mines in the region. They delivered, he didn't. You won't find its other name on any map: Cabo Infierno; lyrical, don't you agree?"

"Cape Hell. It's practically a sonnet."

"In 1519, the disgruntled Aztecs captured several Conquistadors there and put them to death by pouring molten gold down their throats. Clearly, the concept of irony is as indigenous to the New World as the potato."

"Let's hope it hasn't survived as well. I can't swallow even a jalapeno without regret."

"I rather think Captain Childress is at least partially responsible for the endurance of the name. The Pinkerton's report cites rumors of soldiers beheaded for desertion and their bodies turned over to cannibals."

"He got into the tequila. Indians aren't man-eaters."

"I suspect Childress circulated the stories himself. He's established in the local cane sugar trade—that's public record—and when it comes to discouraging competition there's nothing quite as effective as tales of massacre."

"Planting sugar for profit makes sense, if he is raising an army. The kind of men he needs don't fight for love of country."

"That isn't all," he said, helping himself to an unprecedented third helping of spirits; his Presbyterian leanings counseled against them, and he wasn't a hypocrite in practice. "The federales say he grows poppies between the rows."

"Opium."

"The climate is ideal."

I emptied my glass a second time. "The Civil War's starting to be the least interesting part of his biography."

FOUR

The cashier in the Miner's Bank read the draught signed by Judge Blackthorne, then rolled mud-colored eyes above his pinch-glasses to see if I wore a bandanna over my face. I got out the badge I carried in a pocket, showed him my appointment papers signed by U.S. Marshal J. S. Sweeney, waited while he retired behind a door with PRESIDENT painted in black letters on the pebbled glass, pasted on an angelic expression when the man who belonged to the office stuck his head out and studied me head to foot, and walked out a half-hour later, leaving behind my signature on a receipt and carrying two hundred dollars in double-eagles in a canvas sack. I could have robbed the place in half the time and gone off with ten times as much.

Black Dan Stuart ran a stagecoach stop on the Bozeman, supplying the horses himself from his small (five hundred acres) ranch a mile outside Helena. He wasn't any more black than I was: He claimed service with the Scots Highlanders, also called the Black Watch, in the Crimea. I had my doubts, and they were shared; but when he took it into his head to man the way station personally, he greeted dusty travelers in a kilt and tam-o'-shanter, warping their eardrums with a set of bagpipes.

The costume wasn't suited to the local climate in summer, and Marshal Whitsunday had offered to fine him the next time he squeezed his bag of wind within earshot of Helena, so I found him in ordinary canvas and blue flannel and the straw planter's hat he wore when the sun hammered down. He had a mouth somewhere, but the only evidence of it was the almost unintelligible brogue that came out from behind his red mutton-chop whiskers, stirring the silvered tips.

"What's that you're r-r-r-riding, lad?" He stood on his rick-rack porch, thumbs hooked inside the cinch he used to hold up his trousers. "It's too big for a sporting girl and too pr-r-r-retty for a horse."

I stepped out of leather and smacked the pinto mare's neck. It rolled an angry eye my way; I'd yet to make a good first impression on anything that burns hay. "It belongs to Judge Blackthorne's wife. She's too fat to ride it anymore, and too stubborn to sell it. It's a loan until I take possession of that thoroughbred he says you're holding."

"I hesitate to let go of it; but he pr-r-r-romised to let me play at the Independence Day dance."

I thanked God I'd be a thousand miles away by the Fourth.

It was a sound enough beast, a bay with one white stocking and a crescent-shaped blaze. He'd named it after a character he said was in *The Arabian Nights*, but there were a lot of *r*'s in it and he was still rolling them when I left, leading the pinto. Chances were I'd have to shoot it sooner or later and I wasn't about to take time to carve its name on a cross. I swear it: As I topped the first hill, I heard the old fraud serenading me with a wheezy interpretation of "Amazing Grace."

My next stop was the Montana Central yard, and my home-on-rails for the foreseeable future.

At first glance, *El Espanto* disappointed; on a siding near one of Broadwater and Hills' two-story-high locomotives, the engine looked small and quaint, although shiny as bootblack with red trim and its name painted in italics on the wooden cab just beneath the opening where the engineer propped his elbow. It hauled four cars only: the tender heaped with wood, a Pullman parlor car, a stock car, and caboose. No sign of the saloon car Blackthorne had teased me with; he jibed as he ruled in court, without fear of consequences.

At second glance the outfit passed muster. It was short but sturdy, mounted on wheels disproportionate to its size, built to churn their way through floods of muck and mud and blizzards above the tree line, with wicked-looking iron spikes on the cowcatcher, stout enough to impale a buffalo bull and carry it along with all the ease of blown chaff. The *Ghost* it was called, but the name was the only ethereal thing about that outfit.

A caterpillar scampered up my spine then. I was riding the rails into a place called Cape Hell, aboard a train equipped to enter the original.

A squat Indian sat on the edge of the cab with his feet dangling, eating a sandwich and washing it down with something from a canteen; I'll call it water. His hair was cut short, mission-style, and he wore overalls and a checked shirt with a filthy bandanna around his neck, but there was nothing European about his black eyes or blunt features, which looked as if they'd been hacked out by a sculptor who hadn't gotten around to smoothing the edges. I never saw him wear a hat, come driving rain or pounding sun, in all the time I knew him; and as it turned out, I knew him longer than most of the men I called my friends.

"Your pardon, Chief," I said. "Where's the fellow who runs this train?"

"I'm not a chief, Chief. Just the fireman." His English was as good as anyone's, drenched though it was in Spanish pronunciation. "He's in town, getting drunk on anything but mescal, and a bite if there's time."

"I'm your next passenger." I showed him the scrap of tin, which based on his expression had all the effect of Monday turning into Tuesday. "Mind if I look around inside?"

"I'm not paid to mind anything but the firebox."

"Page Murdock," I said, since it looked as if we'd be in close association for a while. "What should I call you?"

He showed me his eyeteeth. "Call me your next of kin."

His name, as it happened, was Joseph. He said he'd snatched it at random from an open book of Scripture when he'd been asked to sign it to a manifest.

The parlor car was as plush as the bedrooms in Chicago Joe's, paneled in sweet-scented cedar (I can't abide the smell to this day) with lace curtains on the windows and armchairs upholstered in supple pigskin. You could lose a boot in the figured carpet. Just for safety's sake I moved the most inviting chair out from under a crystal chandelier, but decided not to get used to it until we were under way; I had enemies in town, and too much comfort tended to dull the fine edge. Behind a gnurled cabinet door I found a dozen bottles of Blackthorne's own label secured by leather straps, with all the accouterments in leaded glass; the old man could be as hard to take as Dr. Pfister's Spirits of Castor Bean, but he was as good as his word.

A dry-sink mounted a mahogany pedestal, lined in mother-of-pearl, equipped with a badger brush, pink Parisian soap, and a pearl-handed razor with a Sheffield-steel blade. Bay Rum to lay the skin to rest. I pulled the cork from the bottle. The contents smelled like an explosion in a field of lime; my eyes watered.

It was my brand, to take the edge off the trail. The Judge had done his homework. In any other case I'd have been flattered.

Another cabinet contained a gun rack stocked with a .45-70 Whitney rifle, a British Bulldog revolver, and a Springfield trap-door shotgun. The first was a dandy long-range weapon, and the belly gun sufficient for close-up work when my Deane-Adams wasn't handy, but the Springfield was available only in 20 gauge, enough to annihilate a jackrabbit but not enough to stop a determined man beyond a hundred feet. I saw Ed Whitsunday's hand in that; town law seldom had to engage the enemy more than the length of a barroom. Worse, the scattergun had only one barrel, which doubled the odds against the man behind it. But since I hadn't even brought up the subject of a scattergun, I didn't plan to kick.

A drawer contained all the ammo I'd need to conquer Mexico, for whatever that was worth. Every time we took it, we seemed compelled to give it back.

Not that I cared for the food. You can do only so much with beans and ground corn, and I'd sampled it all a hundred times over before I traded my lariat for the badge in my pocket.

With that in mind, I flipped up the lid on the zinc larder, and looked at tins of tomatoes, peaches, shredded beef, sweet peas, and baby potatoes. I saw Mrs. Blackthorne's hand in *that.* She was a good enough cook to recognize that importing beans to the Halls of Montezuma was like shipping Studebaker wagons to Detroit. She didn't care for me any more than she did the rest of her husband's crazy-quilt crew, but she was as good a Christian as they came.

More tins, big square ones of coal-oil, lashed inside a cabinet lined in lead. They'd have lit the lamps of China through the next dynasty.

I snatched open other doors. Dozens of jugs of water, drawn from Montana wells, proof against parasites; laudanum, in quantities that would ease the pain of hundreds; yards of gauze, enough to patch the wounds of a regiment; a gallon of iodine, another of alcohol. A leather case, glittering with scalpels, forceps, syringes, and bone saws: *bone saws*. Cold Harbor had been less prepared for casualties. I'd been there, and seen the tent.

I looked, but found no sign of a surgeon packed in salt. Blackthorne had missed a step there.

A pattern was emerging; one I didn't like half so much as the one in the carpet, which had come halfway across the world to settle on a portable floor in Old Mexico.

I investigated further. The stock car had straw and sacks of oats sufficient to feed a string, let alone one thoroughbred. The caboose was a cozy affair, equipped with a bentwood rocker, a ticking mattress on an iron frame, and a rolltop desk, with several decks of cards and a bandbox-new checker set in the drawers.

From food to artillery to medical supplies to diversions, the train was stocked halfway toward the twentieth century.

I made a mental note to bring along *The Odyssey* for entertainment; it might last me to the last stop, if I read it in the original Greek and played a few thousand games of checkers.

I thought I'd snookered the old man out of a case of Scotch whisky and two hundred dollars in gold, but by the time the thing was through I figured I'd be lucky to clear a nickel an hour, not counting doctor's bills, with nothing left to drink but warm beer distilled through the bowels of a burro.

The Honorable Harlan Blackthorne always had the last word. I fancy I hear it whenever I lay flowers on his grave.

FIVE

If I'd learned nothing else during my time with him, I knew better than to expect explanations once I'd accepted an assignment. He'd only give me one of those toothless tight-lipped cat's smiles and say no intelligence was as useful as the kind I found out on my own; Washington jargon for what I didn't know couldn't hurt me. Which was a bald-faced lie, as I'd found out on my own more times than I could count.

So I went over his head, literally: straight to the attic.

Blackthorne had lost patience while the local, territorial, and federal authorities were arguing the details of constructing a courthouse, and had set up shop in the headquarters of the *Herald* building, arranging recesses to coincide with when the presses in the basement began their daily rumble. He'd had the attic cleared of stacks of old numbers of the newspaper to make room for records and evidence, turning it into a combination file room and Black Museum. Trial transcripts rolled and bound with cord stuck out like ancient scrolls from floor-to-ceiling pigeonholes, clamshell boxes stood cheek-by-jowl on freestanding shelves open on both sides, and wooden cases contained case files in leather folders amidst a thicket of edged and percussion weapons hung up like heraldic arms. The collection bore nightmare tales of beheadings, back-shootings, and duels fought at such close range the combatants' shirts caught fire; these, too, dangled from pegs, singed and stiff with old blood, reeking of stale smoke and charred flesh. It all added up to some ten thousand years at hard labor and a potters' field of necks broken on the scaffold.

The curator and headmistress of all this sat at a student desk, her erect back supported by whalebone wrapped in black bombazine and a rimless monocle behind which swam a brown eye swollen all out of proportion, like a fish in a bowl. Just where Electra Highbinder spent the hours of darkness added color to the conversation in Chicago Joe's. Depending on which story you bought, she slept on a cot among the stained broadaxes and jars of poisoned livers or sipped green tea from a translucent cup in a room above the Gans and Klein Clothing Store at Main and Broadway furnished in the Federal style, all carved mahogany eagles and rich leather bindings inside blown-glass presses; this on the authority of the man who'd delivered her four-poster bed from Montgomery Ward.

I followed protocol: Took off my hat, called her Mrs. Highbinder, and stated my request. I had no evidence that she actually refused access to those who got it out of sequence, but the ghost of a husband last seen at the bottom of a shaft in Last Chance Gulch hung about her like tuberose and there was nothing to be gained by stirring him.

"Childress?" She off-loaded one of her plat-book-size ledgers from the stack on the floor by her knee onto the desk, splayed it open, and ran the fletch of her old-fashioned quill down the crowded columns, stopping near the bottom of the page. The quill rose from the sheet, pointing across the room. "CH-17."

I found it among the clamshell boxes on a shelf and started to leave with it tucked under my arm. A rapid clicking noise brought me back around to where she sat tapping the nib of her pen against tea-stained teeth. Again she reversed the quill, lining it up with a writing table standing in a pool of milky sunlight leaking through a fan-shaped window across from her station. The meaning was clear: I could leave, but the box stayed.

The split-bottom chair found every saddlesore I'd accumulated since I'd left Helena the last time, but I opened the box and spilled its contents onto the table. They were in a bundle, tied with more cord. I tugged loose the knot, set aside a ragged stack of newspaper clippings, and began reading a neat clerkly hand on foolscap sheets, identified at the top as a transcription from the decoded report wired by the Pinkerton who'd vanished in Mexico.

His name was DeBeauclair, but he'd walked the length of the Sierra Madre posing as a Portuguese sailor who called himself Salazar, and who'd had his fill of the sea and had pledged to hike through all the uncivilized places of the earth until some vision told him what direction his life should take.

The story was just lunatic enough to satisfy the most suspicious observer. In reality, DeBeauclair/Salazar was working for U.S. banking interests, tracking bandits who'd been raiding the border for months, looking for names and evidence for warrants to extradite. Along the way, he'd picked up on the rumors of Oscar Childress' activities in the interior.

The agent had been sufficiently intrigued to take time out from his original assignment and report what he'd heard through the Western Union office in the anonymous fishing village in Cabo Falso, but according to a letter accompanying the notes, all attempts to reach him afterward had failed. That letter, written on heavy rag bond and addressed to U.S. Attorney General Augustus Garland, bore the disturbing all-seeing eye and "We Never Sleep" pledge of the Pinkerton National Detective Agency, and the signature of Robert A. Pinkerton himself, son of its legendary founder, and every bit the miserable son of a bitch his father had been. He demanded federal intervention. An addendum scribbled in a different hand suggested that the matter "be taken under advisement."

Which explained the letter's presence in Judge Blackthorne's files.

It was dated five months ago, which was standard procedure regarding stories of conspiracy against the Union. They were as cyclical as the tides, and few of them attracted more notice than it took to file them away; but whenever one managed to creep so far north from its origin, the president had to be consulted, and Grover Cleveland was not a man to dismiss such things lightly only four years after the Garfield assassination.

DeBeauclair's report, if it had been disencrypted faithfully, was practical, offering no assumptions beyond what he'd overheard in cantinas and peso-a-week flophouses in coastal villages and witnessed firsthand. The rumors passed without comment; some of them were fantastic on their face, stories of cannibalism and human sacrifice. But he'd read flyers offering top wages for experienced soldiers, preferably without family, seen wagonloads of grim-faced men bound for the Sierras wearing bandoleers of ammunition, rifles and carbines slung from their shoulders, and while passing through a filthy storeroom on his way to an outhouse, staggering convincingly, had lifted the canvas cover off a stack of crates stenciled CUIDADO, and leant down far enough to catch a whiff of sulphur and potassium, the principal ingredients of dynamite. As there was no mining or railroad-building taking place within a hundred miles of the ginhouse, he'd seen fit to include the discovery in his report. Under all these eavesdroppings and observations had run a theme, whispered in disease-ridden brothels, sung in urine-soaked alleys, and spoken in opium trances: "*El General* Childress."

It had taken him almost a quarter-century to overcome his demotion from Union colonel to captain of the Confederacy and promote himself to general.

I turned from the report to the yellowed cuttings, sliced from crumbling copies of *The Charleston Mercury* and *The New York Times,* the leading journalistic voices of the War Between the States. The *Mercury,* a rebel sheet, trumpeted the victories of Childress' volunteers at First and Second Manassas, Chickamauga, and Cold Harbor, while the *Times* made scant reference to an obscure band of southern mercenaries until its commander leapt into its lead column in April 1863:

ATROCITY IN SPRINGFIELD.
Rebel Guerrillas Stop Civilian Train.
Open Fire on Defenseless Passengers.
Eighteen, Including Women and Children, Blasted into Eternity in as Many Seconds.

Accompanying it was a woodcut illustration of a uniformed firing squad with rifles raised, spitting smoke and lead at a reeling line of men in bowlers, women in ankle-length dresses, and children in hair bows and knickers withering before the blast.

Ten minutes later I found a corresponding report in the

Charleston rag, headed SKIRMISH IN SPRINGFIELD. This was a brief account of a battle involving Childress' volunteers and passengers aboard a federal troop train, who had opened fire on the Confederates from onboard. The editors had not elected to provide an illustration.

I'd fought in that war, and had learned, when newspapers were available (usually wrapped around a slab of greasy catfish), that what I'd experienced and what I read about later might have been separate engagements. Throw the *Times*'s massacre and the *Mercury*'s armed encounter into a bushel basket, shake it, draw out your own interpretation, and you might have something approaching the truth. Personally I had trouble singling out a specific act of malice from the general hell of war: The worse it got, the better, if anyone who might wind up in charge had learned anything from it. I was more interested in Cold Harbor, and whether one of the faces I'd looked into across the crossroads that long day, black with powder and striped from sweat, had belonged to Oscar Childress. By that fourth year of fighting, officers' insignia were practically nonexistent among the gray and butternut; their uniforms had gone the way of all shoddy, replaced by Union castoff and motley snatched off clotheslines. I remembered a burly party in a dirty lace camisole and a raddled straw hat with holes cut for an ass's ears, turning back a flank attack with a saber stained crimson to the hilt. He might have been a general.

Cold Harbor, Virginia: Fifteen thousand dead or wounded on the side of the Army of the Potomac, as opposed to two thousand on the other. Of all the forgotten battlefields I had no intention of revisiting, that intersection of twin ruts leading nowhere in particular came in dead last.

The *Mercury* ceased publication when Charleston fell in

February 1865, and no mention of Childress had been preserved from the *Times* after Crook's cavalry set fire to a barn his men had deserted during the retreat from Winchester; two hogs and a goat lost their lives in that action, and their affiliation remained undetermined. The last item, therefore, belonged to a publication with a different typeface whose name wasn't included with the clipping. It was two inches only, and read:

> *Readers of this journal will be relieved to learn that Captain O. Childress, author of the infamous slaughter at Springfield, Missouri, has decamped to Mexico with the remains of his command, and is believed to have thrown in with Emperor Maximilian in defense against revolutionists loyal to former President Benito Juarez. May God in His mercy protect the women and children of New Spain.*

Unless the reporter got things backward, Childress had started out hoping to change his luck by siding with established authority, then turned coat and fought once again with the rebels, this time with better results. If so, his mental prowess lived up to its reputation; but it hadn't outlived the nickname he'd acquired during those eighteen seconds in Missouri.

SIX

Something slid out as I was sorting what I'd read from what I hadn't into separate bundles and landed on the table with a plink. Electra Highbinder glanced up, then returned to the column she was filling in one of her ledgers.

I looked at the wrinkled orange tintype of a callow youth in the tunic of a West Point plebe, fastened at the throat: Faded ink on the back identified the model as Cadet O. Childress. Useless to compare that face, unstamped by time and experience, with the man I'd been sent to investigate, and possibly to eliminate: eyes slightly wolfish over a nose thin as crystal and prim slit of a mouth, the whole supporting a bulbous cranium already pushing through the fine pale hairs that covered it. He'd be bald by now, and an ideal specimen for phrenology considering the size of his brain case. I put the image on the pile of deadwood.

I finished the rest of the material and started packing it up to return to the box. A sheet of onionskin was stuck to the back of one clipping. I peeled it away carefully; it was as thin as a postage stamp and as fragile as a butterfly's wing.

The text started in the middle of a sentence; clearly it belonged to a longer tract. The script was written in red ink, the hand coarse, like something in an exercise book kept by someone who was learning his letters, but the language was fine, as if it had been transcribed into formal English from classical Latin, with the occasional foray into the local dialect; a symptom common to an extended stay in a foreign land. The phrasing was elegant, but by the time I came to the end of each carefully crafted sentence I knew no more about its meaning than I had at the beginning. Like Emerson, it fascinated and at the same time left me lost.

A technical term here and there suggested this was a leaf from Childress' own notes, laying out his theories on exploiting Mexican peasants' awe of us *Norteamericanos* in the national interest: The existing seeds had only to be planted, was what I made of it. In a less distracted frame of mind, I might have been persuaded to accept his argument, except for the cold finger that touched my spine when I took a closer look at *matear* (to plant seeds) and realized what he'd actually written was *matar* (to kill).

I wasn't the only one who'd been taken in by the scrawled Spanish: Judge Blackthorne had said the authorities had been impressed with the proposal to turn the peons' awe of our civilization to national advantage, never suspecting he was recommending their extermination. The word, it was true, was all jagged angles, the *t* uncrossed and the *a*'s open at the top, and smudged by too much handling. It was easy to imagine some bureaucrat, inclined to hope for the best, interpreting it as a harmless reference to growth. For all I knew it was just that, and my own traffic with brutish humanity had tainted my outlook; but I'd never gotten in trouble for thinking the worst.

That brought me to Blackthorne's motive. Had he removed the report from the file in order not to alarm me, and overlooked the last page? He overlooked nothing. Had he left it, probably the most revealing passage of all, as a warning to take care? Not for concerns about myself. He was possessive in regard to all the tools at his disposal, and loath to train a replacement.

The paper smelled of pinon smoke and something bittersweet I could place only by bringing it close to my face and breathing deep: nightshade. Childress had picked berries and crushed them to make the ink.

That provided a picture more vivid than the outdated tintype. I saw him sitting cross-legged in a mud hut, filling page upon page with his fevered scratches, pausing only to dip his pen—a cactus needle or a porcupine quill—in scarlet paste in an earthenware dish. He wore only a loincloth, native headdress, and a snailshell necklace. He'd have gone heathen.

How else explain a man who proposed wholesale massacre as a step toward progress? I had to meet him.

You needed to run a thousand head of cattle minimum to qualify for membership in the Montana Stock-Growers Association, but Harlan A. Blackthorne had never gotten closer than a rare steak in the dining room of the Magnolia Hotel. He'd been granted honorary standing for his legal efforts to defend the open range from an army of lawyers determined to cut it up for the real estate interests back East. Although he had no love for cattle barons, nor they for him—he often ruled in favor of small ranchers in disputes over property lines—he agreed that the grassland was designed by God for grazing and that to plow it under would expose the subsoil to harsh winds and brutal sun, inviting drought. No less an authority than Chester Alan Arthur had tried to intervene on behalf of the New York lobbyists who had kept him in the White House, but like several presidents before him he'd dashed himself to splinters against that rocky shore.

The house had been built by a silver magnate who'd put a ball through his head when his wife left him, taking their daughter and son with her back to New Hampshire. Its turrets and gables, copied from a castle in Sweden, had appealed to another sort of pioneer, and the molded plaster ceilings and cedar paneling were dark with old cigar exhaust and soaked with the sickly sweet stench of Levi Garrett's. The association's founders had turned the old ballroom into a gallery of Remington prints, bought the works of Shakespeare and De Quincey by the pound, and interred them in glazed presses that were opened only by the servants who dusted the uncracked leather spines: The slyest man under that roof could cheat a Vanderbilt, but he couldn't read or write his own name.

The doddering veteran of the War of 1812 who'd kept the registration book in the pink marble lobby had passed finally, and been replaced by an erect young Negro with a British accent and a white eye, who informed me that the Judge was in the gymnasium.

"The bar, you mean," I said.

"No, sir. End of the hall."

I studied his face, planed flat at every angle like the head atop a totem pole. "Didn't you cost me a bundle in the Blessing fight?"

"Blessing made it back. He bet against himself. Not that he didn't try to lose it." He touched the corner of the dead eye.

The gymnasium smelled of good spirits squeezed through sweaty pores. A pair of swollen bellies in padded gear was fencing in the middle of the floor, but neither of them belonged to the Judge. He watched the battle from an oaken bench, both hands wrapped around a silver-plated flask.

I sat down beside him. "Impressive," I said. "Do you think they'll ever replace stone axes?"

"That jackanapes Roosevelt has taken over upstairs, gassing about the strenuous life on his spread in Dakota. While he was about it I watched him polish off two plates of lobsters he had packed in dry ice and shipped all the way from Maine. Then I came down here to watch two old fools play at pirates. You found all the appointments satisfactory?" He waggled the flask, but I held up a palm and handed him the onionskin sheet I'd folded and put in a pocket. He glanced at it and gave it back.

"Ghastly hand; not that it signifies. Graphology is based on the naïve assumption that when the tail of the *g* sweeps too low and the crown of the *d* climbs too high, the one represents melancholy, the other monomania; as if north is up and south is down anywhere but on a map. Poor illumination and haste are discounted."

"You've seen it."

"It was in the envelope with the letter from the attorney general. I haven't decided whether that was deliberate."

"Me, neither. I thought it was you. How's your Spanish?"

"Rusty, same as my skills with a saber; although I flatter myself I could show these moo-cow millionaires a trick or two. You can ask Childress himself if he was referring to gardening or genocide."

"I think you know."

He unstopped the flask and sipped, swallowed.

"Great men are seldom good. Andrew Jackson murdered a man, ostensibly over an affair of honor, turned his back on the Constitution he swore to uphold, and sentenced a peaceful and assimilated tribe of Indians to an eternity in the desert; yet he's celebrated as our greatest president since Washington."

"Jackson never called for wholesale slaughter."

"Didn't he? Two thousand British dead in New Orleans might argue the point. The war had been over for two weeks."

"He didn't know that at the time."

"Perhaps not. I wonder if it would have made a difference if he had. As a general he invaded Florida against direct orders from Washington."

"You're not making much of a case against Childress."

"That's your job. Or *for* him, if the rumors prove false. I asked you if you had everything you needed."

"I inspected the train. You left out cannon."

"Are you complaining that you're overequipped?"

"Undermanned. According to Agent DeBeauclair, he's got dynamite. I don't think he's blasting stumps."

"If you're asking how to do your job, I'm fresh out of ideas."

"I would be, if you meant what you said about investigating the rumors. You'd send Dick Button for that. He worked undercover for Wells Fargo three years. I'm not a detective; I'm a hired gun. I just can't figure out why you don't have Childress brought back and do the thing proper with a rope."

"He'd take the stand in his own defense. You know his reputation. By the time he was through testifying, the jury would nominate him for territorial governor."

"How do you want him?" I asked. "Nailed to the wall of the

president's mansion in Mexico City or dumped down a mine-shaft in Chiapas?"

"It won't matter either way." He looked at me for the first time since I sat down. "It's Mexico, Page. No one cares what happens down there."

SEVEN

I **packed my** biggest valise for a long stay, with plenty of changes and books for every mood, beginning with my Bible, looked around my room as if I'd never see it again—not for the first time—and rode the bay down to the railyard, where I gave a pair of roustabouts a quarter apiece to back it into a stall in the stock car and hobble it. I put my saddle and bridle, my two most valuable possessions, in the private coach with the valise. That made it seem a little more like me.

Back outside I found Joseph the fireman hurling chunks of wood from a wheelbarrow into the tender. I asked him if the engineer was back from town. He jerked his chin toward the locomotive.

A man built nearly as close to the ground, but just as wide, leapt down from inside, wiping his broad broken-nailed hands on a rag and transferring as much grease to his palms as it removed from them. I shook his hand, making sure to give as good as I got; men who spent most of their time gripping steel levers seldom throttled back for flesh and bone.

"Hector Cansado." He had one of those deep, burring voices that came from shouting over a chugging engine. His accent was unconventional, neither Spanish nor Indian; it seemed to have been dropped by accident, borne by some strange bird from terra incognita. He wore the ticking-striped cap, faded red kerchief, and brass-studded overalls of his profession, the heavy denim pitted all over with burns from flying sparks. His broad face, similarly scarred, had a bloated quality, the skin stretched to its limit, like an India rubber balloon, and yellow-green in complexion. Mahogany-colored eyes tilted away from a flat nose, creating an impression of desperate fatigue. Even his name translated as "tired."

He was dying; his coloring suggested advanced jaundice. That cold finger touched my spine again. I was in the hands of a fireman whose ancestors had known nothing but tragedy at the hands of the white race and an engineer who had nothing to lose by piloting a train through darkest Mexico.

His breath stank of sour mash. I asked him if he'd succeeded in finding anything to drink besides mescal and something to eat. The tight face registered annoyance. The weary eyes slid toward the Indian.

"That savage has been carrying tales. What a man does on his own time is his business."

"I guess. I haven't had my own time in ten years. There's good Scotch in the parlor car and not a grain of cornmeal in sight."

"Is this an invitation?"

"We've got a thousand miles to cover. I don't want to lose my company manners out of habit."

He leaned forward and dropped his voice to a murmur.

"Don't tell Joseph. The only time you can trust him is when he is drunk, and then you can trust him to cut your throat."

I glanced at the man throwing wood. "Why do you keep him on?"

"I would rather have him aboard than wonder about him outside in the dark."

"You know where we're headed?"

"Cabo Infierno, *sí*."

"Does Joseph?"

"Not from me, but he has ears to hear and eyes to see, and *El Espanto* is not your ordinary train. I would not put it past him to throw in with that devil."

Under some circumstances I might have considered that a good beginning. Tragedies always start out bright, comedies grim. But life isn't the theater.

Cansado left Joseph to his labor on the pretext of showing me features of the train I'd already seen and joined me in the coach. I tugged the cork out of one of Blackthorne's bottles and poured two inches into each of a pair of cut-crystal glasses and we settled ourselves into the pigskin chairs. He looked around, at the paneling and the rich rugs, shook his head.

"In the village where I was born, the cost of this coach would keep us in meat for a year; beef, I mean. I have eaten so many chickens it is a wonder I do not lay eggs. I have heard they serve tortillas as far north as Santa Fe. I cannot believe this."

"It's worse than that. You can order green chiles in Portland, Oregon."

"Myself, I would travel twice that far to escape them. Someday I shall don a serape and hike toward Canada, and when

I meet the first person who asks me what it is I am wearing, there is the place I will settle."

"Strange talk for a Mexican."

Tired eyes glared at me over the top of his glass. "I am Basque. My people owe loyalty to no one but themselves."

"It sounds lonely."

He drank, wobbled it around his mouth, and swallowed. The played-out gaze remained steady. "I think you know this feeling."

"I travel with friends." I set down my drink, got up, unstrapped the valise, and took out the Bible. "Mark, Matthew, Luke, Ezekiel. I call them by their first names. They go where I go."

"And should the book be lost or stolen?"

I tapped my chest with a corner. He shrugged.

"Myself, I have no friends, dead, canonized, or other. It is why I took this job. No other would accept it, once they heard where this train was bound."

"Are all your colleagues so superstitious?"

"Demons are easy. There are spells, talismans. It is not so with men. I see you know nothing of the Mother Range."

"I've climbed the Bitterroots and crossed the Divide. One set of mountains is much like all the rest."

He drew a jagged line through the condensation on his glass with a forefinger. "You have heard the story of how Cabo Infierno got its name?"

"I have. The Spanish demanded gold; they forgot to say how they wanted it delivered. I don't fear places named for hell or the devil or death. It's men who named them."

"You talk as one who never laid eyes on the devil."

I resumed my seat, the Bible in my lap, and picked up my glass. "I suppose you're going to tell me you have."

"Not I. But then I have not had the privilege of meeting Oscar Childress. Have you angered your superiors, that you should be sent to the Sierras?"

"I volunteered."

"You seek your death willingly?"

"No one has ever done that. Even men who jump off bridges must have second thoughts just before the end. Everything I hear about Childress convinces me I'd be missing something if I passed up the chance to meet him face-to-face."

"I am certain that is what Montezuma said about Cortes."

He doubled over suddenly, hugging himself; then just as quickly recovered, sat back, and resumed drinking. I realized then that he'd been in constant pain, and that the spasm had only been the worst in an unbroken line.

I felt a sudden rush of pity; it was probably the whisky. "What is your affliction, my friend?"

"My liver. Too much tequila and mescal, not enough grapefruit and apples. The doctor in Durango allowed me a year, the shaman in Quezalcoatl three months. I should have quit after the first." He raised his glass. "I drink to my liver, for bringing me this far. I have never been north of La Junta." He emptied it and stood. "Thank you for the excellent spirits. We must be on our way. I am told an express is coming through."

"It's not due until four o'clock. There's time for another. Unless—" I made a gesture in the direction of his misery; or where I thought it might be. I knew next to nothing of the bodies I'd sent to the grave.

"The damage is done; I speak not of that nor of the hour. I must ask you to take care that one of us remain sober at all times."

"We're a long way from the Sierras."

"We shall speak again of that subject, when I explain to you the rules. Meanwhile I cannot predict what Joseph would do if he found both of us *borracho.* I trust him no more than my liver." He left me to my drink and my Holy Writ.

EIGHT

Working up a head of steam, the boiler sent a pulse the length of the train, like a horse bunching its muscles for a long gallop. The delay between the pull of the tender and the reaction by the coach was like a gasp for breath. In the weeks ahead I would come to regard that arrangement of bolts, plates, pistons, and couplers as a living thing, and when I slept—which is how I recommend traveling through most of Utah and Arizona—to fancy that I was an extension of it, my veins and arteries connected with it the way Barnum's Siamese twins were each physically dependent on the other; the churning of the drive-rods melded with the beating of my heart, the rhythmic wheezing of steam and smoke with the function of my lungs. When Hector Cansado blew the whistle at crossings, I felt its hoarse shrill bellow in my testicles. We were one and the same, the *Ghost* and I.

From Great Falls to Tucson, we stopped at the same place to

take on water and wood: the long low frame station, the loafers holding up its porch roof with their shoulder blades, the slouch-hatted driver handling the reins of the team hitched to a dray carrying its cargo of barrels down a cross street strung together with all the others. I manufactured names for all of them, man and beast, the closest friends I'd had in a long while. I ate chicken and dumplings twenty times in the Bluebell Café, served by a substantially built woman named Martha, drank coffee that had been boiling since dawn. One tree had provided all the apple pies, the crusts burnt in a black crescent. In each place, the talk was of a farmer kicked by a mule, a little girl drowned in a well, a midwife hacked to pieces and distributed alongside a mile of county road. The victims were interchangeable, but the mayhem followed the theme as before. A man named Gus would hang a hundred times.

I don't know when the engineer slept, or if he did at all; maybe, aware of how little time he had left, he'd decided not to waste any of it insensible, dozing in snatches at the throttle, close enough to the surface to react to sharp bends, steep plunges, and obstacles on the tracks. Apart from that—if even that—he took his rest with me in the private car while Joseph tended the boiler at rest, drinking a hole in Judge Blackthorne's private stock, sometimes joining me in a hand of poker, playing with matchsticks and swapping biographies.

He was the eldest of eleven, not counting one miscarriage, two stillbirths, and a sister who died of diphtheria at the age of two weeks. His mother took in washing, and his father had spent a total of six hours with his children, leaving their one-room hut before sunup and chipping bits of color out of granite until the coal-oil ran out around midnight.

"We had a good working system," he said. "Mama would take a turtle from a trap in the river and I would stand on its shell while Felipe applied pliers to its jaw, pulling out its head, Alessandro chopped it off, and Delores snatched it by its tail and threw it into a boiling kettle. You know turtle soup?"

I nodded. "In San Francisco. They called it terrapin in the Bella Union."

"Snapper, we. I learned to avoid the severed head at an early age, when a hen pecked at it out of curiosity and it locked onto the bird's throat. They will hold on, you know, until sundown, or until the brain gets the message that it is no longer connected to the body. Pass the bottle, *senor, por favor.*

"Ah! To have discovered such nectar years ago would have been worth my liver. It was an important moment in my passage when I was declared old enough, first to use the pliers, then to swing the axe. What I would not give to eat turtle soup once again. The river was fished out long ago."

"And what of Felipe, Delores, and the rest?" I asked.

He set a matchstick to use, igniting a cigarette he rolled himself in brown paper. The smoke from the scorched grain made me lightheaded, an argument in its favor; liquor benefited no one but the drinker.

"*Quien sabe?* The soldiers came for Alessandro to help them fight for Maximilian; we never heard from him again. Then more soldiers came for Felipe to help them fight for Juarez. We heard he was shot for desertion. Delores became pregnant by the son of a don and was sold to a brothel. I do not know what became of the child. The *rurales* arrested me when I trespassed upon the don's ranch. They took away my rifle, which was fifty years old and did not work anyway, and I was sentenced to labor in the same mine that claimed my father's life when it fell in, along with those of a dozen others.

"I served with the crew that excavated it. I do not know which of the skeletons we uncovered belonged to my father.

I would be working there still if a man representing railway interests in *Los Estados Unidos* hadn't come looking for a fireman to replace the one he'd lost when a boiler exploded near Chihuahua; he was blasting tunnels for a line to be owned jointly by the Oklahoma, Texas, and Missouri Railroad and the government in Mexico City. I had just started as an engineer when *El Presidente* Diaz nationalized the railway in the interest of the Republic. *Lo mismo, senor, por favor.*"

I refilled his glass. He'd drunk half a bottle to two drinks on my part without affecting either his speech or his reflexes.

He sipped, sighed. "When we were grading track not far from my old village I chanced to look in upon the home where I grew up. Strangers were living there, and knew nothing of the former occupants. It is a trial, *Senor* Deputy, to visit a bordello and not know if one is lying with one's own niece."

I had nothing to offer in comparison with his experiences. I'd been shot, almost burned to death, lured into traps by evil women, and spent a season as a slave with Cheyenne renegades, but I had nothing to match his loss.

That is, if he was telling the truth. If I had a cartwheel dollar for every Mexican whose sister had been raped by a Spanish don, I could have spent my life traversing the continent in a private railway car.

Joseph was a puzzle of another sort. I doubt we exchanged more than fifty words total, most of them monosyllabic and unrevealing, but even before we left Montana Territory I was convinced he was some kind of Judas goat, leading us toward a slaughterhouse. He spent all his time in the locomotive when he wasn't foraging for fuel—not overlooking the merest scrap of driftwood on the shore of the Great Salt Lake or mesquite twig in the Painted Desert—crunched down cracked corn by the handful, chasing it with water from a goatskin bag, and crossed himself before he ate, clutching the carved-stone crucifix suspended from the rosary around his neck. For all his show of Christian conversion, I pictured him more easily offering morsels to a beast-headed god squatting in some undiscovered ruin, praying for our destruction.

The *Ghost* passed through city and plain, leaving no more evidence of its passage than would its namesake. Most unscheduled journeys by rail fostered a host of gossip, and questions at every stop. The endless chain of Marthas set before me bowl after bowl of chicken and dumplings—scrawny prairie hen, and blobs of mealy flour swimming in grease—with only the usual tinned cheer and no apparent curiosity as to where I was bound and why. There was nothing furtive about it, only a complacency I'd never witnessed before. No one asked me about the news from up north, yet I sensed no hostility, no reticence. I was a piece of furniture, and nothing so interesting as a piano or a new kind of plow.

Out of duty I put in to post offices along the way, in case Blackthorne had wired further instructions or calling for a progress report, only to meet blank faces and shaking heads. Either I'd been forgotten—written off, as a bad debt—or the Judge was laying the groundwork for a plea of ignorance when the mission went sour. I was as much an orphan as Hector Cansado, whose brothers and sisters had been taken from him as by the unfeeling wind.

No, nothing so substantial as an orphan. I was a phantom, like the train I rode, drifting through human bodies, constructions of wood, brick, and adobe, like a mist, only without the chill that came with it. There was no evidence that I existed. Outside Yuma, an antelope grazing next to the cinderbed didn't raise its head as the train swept past within inches. As the animal dissolved in a wave of heat I put my hand to my mouth and bit hard into the tender flesh between my thumb and forefinger, and waited for the blood to come to the surface. When it did, proving something, I knew not what, I cracked open my Bible and read:

> *Yet he shall perish forever like his own dung; they which have seen him shall say, Where is he?*
>
> *He shall fly away as a dream, and shall not be found; yea, he shall be chased away as a vision of the night.*

I slammed the book shut. Who wrote this thing, anyway?

I worked my way back to the stock car, bracing myself against the arid wind that struck me like a sheet of superheated iron on the verandah; it stood my skin-cells on end and crackled the hairs in my nose. The wheatgrass stretching to the horizon laid down in the opposite direction the train was headed, making me dizzy. The world was spinning away from me, the ultimate rejection.

The bay lifted its wedge-shaped head when I came through the door, studying me first with one eye, then turning to confirm what it had seen with the left, like a bird on a perch. I strapped on its feedbag and stroked its neck; it lunged, trying to bite me through the canvas. I found that reassuring. Horses still hated me; proof that I was flesh and not air.

I had a strange sensation—a waking dream, like the wisp of unreality that told you you'd been dozing, even when you were struggling with sleeplessness—that I was looking at Lefty Dugan, the friend I'd killed in Butte.

Is that what you thought? he seemed to be saying. *It's the other way around, Page. I killed* you.

Nothing had changed: Shoot one old partner to death and he never let you forget it.

NINE

The time has come," the walrus said, "to speak of rules."

The walrus in this case being Hector Cansado. I'd drunk myself into an Aberdeen stupor, with *Alice in Wonderland* splayed facedown on my chest and a touch of malaria, and awoke to a visage that lacked only whiskers and tusks to fulfill the dream.

"*Senor,*" the engineer said, "We are in Mexico. But where we go, there are no *fiestas,* no *pinatas,* no pretty *senoritas* dancing barefoot upon tables. Nothing you have learned from the past applies to the place we are bound."

"I've been to Mexico before."

"I am sure you had your picture struck in Mexico City, wearing a sombrero and sitting upon a stuffed burro. Where we go, they know nothing of cameras or the telegraph. Men have been slain there for their watches; not to sell, but to take apart and see how they work. They mark the passage of time by the sun and the seasons. The sun sets early in the mountains and rises late, and what happens in between wears the cloak of night. It is no mystery how grotesque stories flourish there.

"Trust no one, least of all your friends. That is rule number one.

"Trust not yourself. Reason and insanity are not so easy to separate in the Mother Mountains: Down is up, dark is light, crooked straight. That is rule number two."

"How many more are they?" I asked. "Should I take notes?"

"Ignore all rules. That is rule number three, and the last I shall give you."

"Was this conversation necessary at all?"

He shrugged. His people were experts at that. "Perhaps not. *Mi madre,* rest her soul"—he crossed himself—"said you cannot know a man until you have seen him in his nightshirt."

I sat up in my berth. "Where are we now?"

"The village of Alamos, in the Sonoran Desert. I suggest you take it in. It is the last civilization we shall encounter this side of Cabo Falso."

I dressed and went outside. The *Ghost* snorted rhythmically, pausing between exhalations, like a stallion bred for racing champing before the gate. Joseph sat as I had first seen him, feet dangling outside the cab, foraging in his sack of corn. His black eyes were more opaque than usual, like wax drippings; either he was relieved to be back on home ground or he'd sweetened his meal with leaves from the plants that grew in lush patches on the sides of the foothills beginning just steps from the train, their distinctive five-leaf clusters stirring in the slight breeze. I remembered what Blackthorne had said about Childress and his poppies growing between rows of sugar cane. They would thrive in that climate, like the marijuana. No country was better suited for cultivating human vice.

The village, as old as any in North America, sprawled at the very foot of the Sierra Madres. It was as if one of the ancient gods had tilted the earth at a seventy-degree angle, and everything on it had slid into a jumble at the bottom. Some of the adobe structures were the oldest in appearance, the original surfaces beaten hard as concrete and covered with patches on patches, each smear a darker shade than its predecessor. The territorial movement had modified later constructions, the windows framed with pinon wood and roof poles extending two feet beyond the walls, looking like elephants' tusks sawn off blunt. Signs identifying the businesses—CORREO, HERRERIA, CARNICERIA—were painted directly on the adobe. More recent buildings were built of pine carted down from just below the tree line and put up green, a blessing during the hot months, when cross-breezes swept through the spaces between the boards, but a curse in monsoon season; inside they would smell of moss and mold and breed mosquitoes the size of sparrows.

A priest leaned in the doorway of the chapel, which although built of the inevitable adobe sported an outer shell of polished limestone, a gleaming white phantom in a world of brown earth. Although he wore the surplice and robes of his calling, his attitude, anticipating something he dared not hope for, a soul saved or a miracle granted, put me in mind of a butcher awaiting his next customer. His gray face brightened as I drew near, only to settle into resignation as I passed, smiling with my lips tight. His faith wasn't mine; I felt no need for an intermediary between myself and my God.

Drinking locally brewed beer in the cantina, dark and damp as a grotto, I heard a loud plop and rescued a woolly caterpillar from drowning among the hops floating in my glass.

I didn't tarry. In winter, gringos would migrate to that climate like swallows, but with the heat rising in twisting ribbons from the beaten earth of the street, mine was the whitest face in the room, and I was still burned as dark as cherry from riding the width of Montana Territory and back. The bartender—a full-blooded Yaqui, judging by his flat features and eyes like shards of polished coal—kept a machete slung by a sinew thong from the wall above the taps, and it didn't strike me as just a decoration.

I tossed some change on the bar, but as I made my way out I saw a rectangular sheet posted next to the door, as brown and wrinkled as cigarette paper, with a woodcut reproduced in black ink of a man in the uniform of a Mexican *federale*: khakis, Sam Browne belt, knee-length boots, schoolboy cap with its shiny leather visor, tearing the clothing from a terrified-looking *senorita,* and a legend I preferred to translate into English when I wasn't among witnesses. I pretended to stumble, bumping against the wall, and held up a hand to my audience, reassuring them of my welfare, as with the other I tore the sheet off its nail and stuffed it into a pocket.

VOLUNTEERS WANTED! [It read]
TOP WAGES!
FIGHT FOR FREEDOM, FAMILY, LAND
SEE PROPRIETOR FOR DETAILS
OSCAR CHILDRESS, MAJOR,
THE ARMY OF LIBERTY

I showed it to Cansado when he reported to the coach for his regular session with Scottish skullbender. He stared at it, said:

"This same picture accompanied *El Presidente* Juarez's leaflets at the time of the revolution. Alas, I was pressed into service before I learned my letters."

I made him a beneficiary of my incomplete Spanish. He nodded.

"Ah. No monetary inducements were offered then. Had they been, it may not have been necessary to recruit my brother at the point of a bayonet."

"Correct me if things have changed since my last visit, but isn't this evidence in favor of a firing squad?"

"It is, perforce. But we are many miles from the capital, with many more to travel, most of them vertical, and steep canyons whose floors the sun has never reached. Many things lurk there, *Senor* Deputy, some with a hundred legs, and poison enough to paralyze a regiment. However, it is my observation that the danger increases as the number of legs wane, until one is left with but two, that march to the beat of General Childress' drum."

I tilted my glass, pointing its rim at my companion. "Don't be insulted, but you're a liar. No illiterate can spout such poetry merely from the hearing."

The yellow bloated face showed no offense. "Is it not wise, sometimes, to feign ignorance, in order to barter time while your foe seeks to educate you?"

"I don't know what you're talking about."

He hesitated, turning over the words; then grinned for the first time, looking like a jack-o'lantern on November first. He handed back the flyer.

"I fail to see that this is of use. You knew of this already, from the American detective's report. Surely you did not doubt its existence."

"He neglected to include a point of contact. Have you tried the local beer? The caterpillar I fished out of it seemed none the worse for swimming in it."

"Why drink that swill when you have—?" He paused

with his glass half-raised. He set it down gently, his eyes fixed on mine. They had a strange quality, like the brother's I'd never had.

"This bartender," he said, "will direct you to a lonely spot, where you will be assassinated, stripped of your clothes and skin, and dragged still living behind an oxcart, and then they will fry your entrails and serve them up with the local beer."

"The hell you say. Indians don't eat human flesh."

"Did I say anything about Indians?"

He was difficult to fathom. How did a man, whose entire life had been lived south of La Junta, know so much about the depths to which humans could sink? Just seeing his family decimated by continuous revolution didn't answer. Some men are born already old in the ways of the wicked world.

"You're forgetting what I have to offer," I said.

"*Dinero?*" He drank, snorted Scotch out his nose, wiped his face on his sleeve. "*Banditti* apprehended with American gold coins are shot without trial, the gold divided among the arresting officers; these brigands would sooner handle a rattlesnake. Weapons? They will raid this car upon your death and confiscate them all."

He shook his head. "You *Norteamericanos* are all the same. You think what you own is what you are. You can take nothing from these people that they haven't lost already, including their lives."

"I have one thing they can't have, without the skills to use it," I said, "and that, my friend, is your own ticket to life."

He drank, swallowed. "Now it is you who spouts poetry. What can you possibly give them that they cannot take?"

I settled back in soft pigskin and gestured with my glass, taking in the coach, and by extension the *Ghost* itself.

"As a wise man once said, no revolutionist would be caught dead without a train."

He set down the rest of his drink, rose, smoothed his overalls with all the care of a New York robber baron tugging down his white waistcoat.

"I am not a slave, *senor,* to be sold with the machine I am employed to operate. You may make your terms with Joseph; but he knows little more about the whims of this particular conveyance than you."

"You picked a hell of a time to quit."

"No more so than the time you chose to tell me of your plan. You knew of this in Montana?"

"I did. I had no way of knowing you weren't aware of it yourself."

He sighed; he did it as well as he shrugged.

"It is ever thus. The peon need not be consulted as to his fate."

I drained my glass, filled it again, and tipped the rest of the bottle into his.

"I'm consulting you now. If you refuse, I have no choice but to turn back. A train's no good without the man who knows how to run it."

"What is that to me? Your people are amateurs at war. My country has been at it since Cortes. Should I care whether Chester Cleveland or Oscar Childress is in charge of *Los Estados Unidos*? I have seen emperors and presidents rise and fall, and I am not yet forty years of age. I shall see many more, and yet my people will remain in the same sorry state as they were at the beginning." He spread his palms. "What have I to gain?"

"You've mixed up Chester Arthur with Grover Cleveland."

"No more so than those who have the privilege of voting."

"You're going about it all wrong," I said. "What more have you to lose?"

"My life."

"Spent doing what? Carrying passengers from here to there and back? I saw cable cars doing just that in San Francisco. Where do you end? Where you started."

I stirred my drink with a finger. "Cape Hell, they call the place we're headed. I should have asked you about that back in Helena, as an expert. I can't think of any kind of damnation that didn't put you back where you were in the beginning."

He picked up his glass, swirled the contents, looked into them, like a gypsy reading leaves in an empty teacup.

"You make an interesting point, *Senor.* I cannot help but think that one way or the other leads to death."

I raised my glass. "To death. It's the debt all men must pay."

"*Por que no?*" He raised his. "I for one always feel relieved once I have settled a bill."

TEN

The door at the front of the car opened. Joseph in his overalls stood silhouetted dimly against the rear of the black tender, the white rectangle in his hand startlingly bright in the light of the lamps. It was a recent arrival, obviously. Nothing in his world of smoke, cinders, and grease remained unstained for more than a few minutes.

"For him." He pointed a corner of the envelope at me. "It came just now by a messenger."

He stepped forward to hand it to me. An awkward moment passed during which the engineer and I sat unmoving, waiting. Presently the fireman withdrew, drawing the door shut behind him.

The envelope, in silk bond, was addressed to me in neat copperplate, sealed with a blob of black wax and the letters K.G.C. pressed into it, probably by a signet ring, in the center of an oak-leaf cluster. I showed it to Cansado.

"I do not know these initials," he said.

"Knights of the Golden Circle. They spied in the North for the Confederacy during the war." I broke the seal, and read, in the same tidy hand on matching stationery:

Dear Mr. Murdock:
I represent the legal interests of General Oscar Childress, and would consider it a great favour if you would honor me with your presence in my quarters this evening.

A card engraved on heavier stock of the same quality was clipped to the page, replicating the name the writer had signed and his address:

Felix Bonaparte, Esq.
No. 9 Calle Santa Anna
Alamos, Mexico

"This name is French, is it not?"

"It might explain his connection with the K.G.C.," I said. "France sided with the rebels."

"It may be a trap."

"Probably." I rose, rummaged among the artillery in the drawer of the gun rack, and buckled on the Deane-Adams.

"Shall I go with you?"

"No. The only thing I brought of any value is this train. If I gave them the man who knows how to run it, I'd be hailed as a hero of the Confederacy."

"I keep a pistol in the cab. Not even Joseph knows about it."

I got out the Springfield shotgun, laid it across his lap, and handed him a box of shells. "There's no telling how many might come. If you let them get close enough, you can take out several at a time. Do you know—?"

Before I could finish, he opened the trap-door action, poked a shell into the chamber, and slammed it shut. He smiled at my expression. "No, *senor,* I have never held this weapon. It is a poor engineer who can examine a piece of machinery and fail to determine how it works."

I spread my hands. "Then I'm away."

"*Senor* Deputy. Page." He stood, foraged in a pocket of his overalls, and came up with an image of St. Christopher embossed in bronze at the end of a chain. "This was a gift of my grandmother, the day I left the village in which I was born. It has seen me through these many years."

I reached to take it. He snatched it back against his breast. His lips twisted.

"Do you think, upon the basis of some nights spent in drink, I would give this to you?—this, of all things? I wished merely to say that I hoped you owned something in which you found the same measure of protection."

I grinned. "You son of a bitch."

"*Sí.*" He returned the token to its pocket. "I have this same information from the man I called my father, on his deathbed, where lies are useless. The knowledge of my bastardy by nature gives me a certain advantage over those who must earn the distinction by conduct."

I unholstered the English revolver, spun the cylinder, twirled it back into leather, patted my Bible, and put it in the side pocket of the frock coat I wore in civilization with the same flourish. "What the one cannot deliver, so the other shall."

Something approaching a wrinkle creased the tight expanse of his forehead. "Mark? Matthew?"

"Murdock."

"Ah. A book yet to be written; had I but my letters." He refilled his glass.

A hag draped in tatters, with a tin tiara gleaming in the rats of her hair, knew El Calle Santa Anna, and offered to take me there for the price of an American dollar. She'd have known me for what I was even if I'd worn a filthy serape and a tattered sombrero; they can smell it. A year saturated in fried peppers, cornmeal, and rapid immersions in leechy creeks would hardly have been enough to wash away the gringo. When, nearing the corner, she backed into a dark doorway and raised her skirts, hoping to raise the ante, I thanked Christ for the darkness, slipped another half-dollar into her crusted palm, and shoved away from her. Her parting cackle interrupted itself long enough only to bite into the coin. I'd have trusted her rotting incisors over any assayer's scale when it came to separating silver from lead.

The street had been laid out under the early Spanish colonists, with no thought of anything broader than a dogcart passing through. At times the way was so narrow I couldn't have stumbled over one of the many uneven stones and fallen as far as the ground; a scraped shoulder was as much as I'd get, and the devil of a time prying myself loose to proceed. As the way grew darker and tighter, I had to concentrate to avoid confusing horizontal with vertical, and thinking I was climbing the inside of a chimney. The soot was as thick, and the path as black.

Not all of the buildings bore numbers. I had to strike a match to read the addresses that existed, some painted directly on the lintels above the sunken doors, others, harkening back to a more genteel past, enameled in flaked paint on the pebbled-glass panels of coach lamps, most of them dark and colonized by wasps, sleeping in their paper cells. A rat crossing the alley paused on my instep, its eyes glowing red by matchlight, then humped along the rest of its way. I was the trespasser, but not one worth challenging.

No. 9, when it revealed itself, was something apart from its surroundings. The street broadened just before I came upon it, like a forest clearing in a fairy tale, with the witch's house nestling quietly in its center, all brown sugar and molasses with a roof made of shortbread.

It wasn't quite that; two stories built in the Tudor style, mortar and timber, oak shutters pierced with holes just wide enough to expel and repel bullets. It was of more recent construction than the rest of the village, but created the impression of something older, harkening back to a time of medieval siege. The prosaic sign stretching the length of the street front belonged to a time neither of the building's inspiration nor of its surroundings:

BONAPARTE & SONS

SOLICITORS

A large bronze bust of Napoleon in his cocked hat shared a plate-glass window with a group photograph on a small easel of the justices of the U.S. Supreme Court, embalmed in stiff collars and moustache wax. A lamp burning deep in the interior shone through the picture, making the judicial branch of the federal government appear transparent.

The door swung open away from my raised knuckles, framing a small man in a black cutaway and a white cutthroat collar. My other hand tightened on the butt of the revolver, but his hands were empty and he was alone in the room. I relaxed my grip.

His clean-shaven face was as brown as a bottle. I assumed

at first that it was the contrast that made his linen seem spotless, but as he pivoted in the direction of the door, beckoning me past him with a dusky palm sticking out of four inches of starched cuff, the inside light fell full upon him and revealed a coat brushed to a bright sheen, a copper-colored necktie snugged tight without a dimple or a scrap of lint, square-toed boots like polished obsidian, and a shirt that would pass muster at a White House state dinner.

He did not shake my hand, but when the door was shut behind him snapped a bow, exposing a round patch of pink scalp in the middle of close-cropped hair, with his thumbs parallel to the seams of his trousers. "Felix Bonaparte, *Monsieur,* and your servant."

His voice was a mild tenor, touched with an accent I associated with the French Quarter of New Orleans. How a Creole had come to light in a village perched on the ankles of the Sierra Madre was as much a mystery as how he managed to support such linen in that climate. The first was none of my business, but I couldn't resist asking about the second.

"The widow two streets over was born in Shanghai, of a Spanish missionary and a *fille de joie.* An aunt shipped her to the New World at the time of the 1864 rebellion, for her safety. San Francisco was the destination, but the navigator was blown overboard in the same typhoon that altered the vessel's course. I can but assume that God intended for me to keep up appearances in this barbaric country. My credentials, you see, are not honored north of the border."

He'd managed to satisfy my curiosity in less than a hundred words. If he could settle all my questions in such short order, the American Bar Association had missed its bet in denying him permission to practice law.

He circled the room, turning up other lamps until the walls

were visible, wainscoted halfway to the ceiling, with more pictures leaning out from the walls, suspended by wires to a rail. They were the usual three-quarter portraits of men in fierce whiskers and black broadcloth, one-eared representatives of eastern schools and northern authority, glowering down on the usual office furniture of oak and maple and overstuffed leather. A plate of beans and a half-eaten tortilla occupied the copper-cornered blotter on the desk.

Bonaparte caught the direction of my gaze. "Have you dined?"

It struck me just then that I hadn't. I was hungry enough to sample the local fare, but wasn't sure how well it would sit on a reservoir of beer and Scotch. I said I was fine.

"You will pardon me, then. I received a packet of material by the morning train, and at such times I frequently work straight through breakfast and dinner. I am anemic, you see. The head, it spins." He gestured toward one of his temples, sat behind the desk, tucked a napkin the size of a tablecloth under his excellent collar, and began scooping beans into his mouth with the skill of someone born to the process without utensils. "I must ask your pardon as well for the lateness of the hour. That same work prevented me from issuing the invitation sooner."

I sat in a tufted love seat facing him. "I don't work by the clock myself. I can't imagine what business you and I have to discuss. I haven't come all this way to enter into any legal agreement."

"Your business is decidedly not legal." He chewed, swallowed, touched a corner of the napkin to each lip-corner, and chased the mouthful with water from a glass goblet. "Everyone in Alamos knows you have come to kill General Childress. It is my responsibility to turn you from this path."

II

The Mother Mountains

ELEVEN

"**Do not insult** us both by denying the fact," Bonaparte said; although if he was any kind of lawyer he wouldn't know by my reaction that I had any such intention. I'd spent too much time in Judge Blackthorne's courtroom, being turned on the spit by defense attorneys, to change expressions. "A stranger cannot cross the border unnoticed, dragging his mission behind him as clearly as smoke from the stack of your splendid train. I myself have lived here nearly twenty years, and when someday I am found extinct at this desk, the publisher of the village newspaper, who is my oldest friend, will write a stellar account of my life, adding that this late arrival will be missed in this village."

I watched him scoop the last of the beans into his mouth, repeating the ritual with his napkin and glass of water. *Joseph,* I thought. The messenger who had brought Bonaparte's invitation was a phantom; the fireman had lost no time reporting to Childress' representative, and been asked—politely, of course—to wait while the lawyer drafted his note. Even George Pullman's superior standards couldn't construct a private parlor coach with walls so thick they'd foil a determined eavesdropper. Had he tried, no less than three locomotives would be needed to pull it.

"You've heard the rumors," I said.

"General Childress would not be the extraordinary man he is if legends did not grow up round him like desert flowers after a spring rain. As with all great men, it is necessary to discount a third of them as invention, another third as either exaggeration or monstrous distortion, and to assign truth to the rest.

"That he intends to liberate this country at last, most definitely. That he is a traitor"—thin shoulders rose above his pristine collar—"must be left to history. Washington and Jefferson were both marked for the gibbet had they failed to repel the British from their shores."

"Since you know so much about me, you must know also that I'm not interested in history lessons."

He sat motionless; but whether he was turning over what I'd said or planning his next move didn't make it as far as his bland placid face. He knew his own way around a courtroom, it seemed.

At length he stirred; I flexed the knuckles of the hand resting on the thigh nearest the Deane-Adams. But all he did was lift a small copper bell from the desk and shake it once. The tinkle was discreet, like everything else about him.

A door opened at the back of the room. I gripped the butt of the revolver; only to relax once again when a boy entered in white cotton peasant dress and sandals. He couldn't have been older than ten, with straight black hair cut square across his brows. Bonaparte spoke to him in clipped tones, in Spanish so rapid I couldn't catch it. The boy withdrew, to return a moment later carrying a leather folder bound with a cord and placed it on the desk. He was dismissed with a snap of the hand.

Bonaparte went on in his pleasant company voice, as if there'd been no interruption, untying the cord as he spoke.

"Do not think that I shall warn the General of your coming. There is no telegraph to his plantation, and the bandit situation is such at present that no mounted messenger would accept the commission. At all events he is prepared perpetually for contingencies of every sort. It is you who should be warned."

"*Merci, Monsieur.*"

"Ah! *Parlez-vous?*"

"*Un petit*. I spent a season in San Francisco."

"A cosmopolitan city, I am told." He removed a bundle of paper from the folder and sorted it into stacks on the desk. His fingers were long, spatulated at the tips, and moved with the swift grace of a skilled faro dealer. "Yes, a most extraordinary man, the General; though he himself prefers the humbler rank of major. These are his papers, which I hope someday to donate to your Library of Congress, and ask no more than a footnote identifying myself as the contributor. Men such as I can hardly expect glory beyond that reflected from the blaze of the truly great."

I watched mesmerized as he placed portions of Childress' meteoric life into prosaic piles, according to his file-clerk's sense of order.

"Your client conducts most of his affairs with the outside world through Cabo Falso," I said. "How can you represent him from five hundred miles away?"

"I agree the situation has difficulties. That I remain alive is not one of them." He continued his activity, cutting no-doubt revealing documents like a deck of cards. "I am not courageous, like you. It is a failing, yes, but one over which I have no control. Would you condemn me if I were born without an arm or with my heart on the wrong side of my chest? It is the same, an unintentional omission on the part of our Lord. Cabo Falso is a nest of pirates and worse. A man of my sort would not survive a week. The General understands this, and thinks no less of me, because I am so much better equipped to deal with paperwork quite as crucial as fertilizer and harvesting equipment. It requires a measure of courage, I assure you, to take a dispatcher to task for a serious error in shipment."

He described his situation so practically I felt ashamed of my own lack of cowardice.

I reflected on what he'd said about fertilizers and harvesting equipment. "He's keeping up the pretense of producing sugar?"

"There is no pretense about it; quite the reverse. He produces more sugar than his five closest competitors combined. You are aware of the importance of bones in the refining process?"

"I hunted buffalo, and saw pickers collecting the bones. They sold them to manufacturers in Detroit, who ground them into powder and ran raw sugar through them to take out the impurities. The bottom fell out of that market with the buffalo."

"He's found a substitute; or another method every bit as good. His merchandise is sought after in all the best restaurants in *Los Estados Unidos* and as far away as Paris, France, so I am told. It is nearly as fine as flour, but superior in granule texture, refusing to clump under the most humid conditions.

Master chefs in the tropical colonies have threatened to resign if their employers will not agree to pay thrice as much for what Childress produces. You have seen his label, perhaps? The armored head of a knight circumscribed by gold laurels?"

Whereupon the son of a bitch turned his lapel, showing me a pin bearing the embossed emblem of the Knights of the Golden Circle. I kept my temper.

"And his opium? Is the quality as good?"

If I'd disappointed him by failing to rise to the bait, he didn't show it; I'd have been disappointed myself if he had. He dropped the lapel back into place and continued sorting, calm as a stone in moonlight. I had his measure now. A poker face is only so good as the amount of pressure you applied to it. When it blew, it would shake the earth.

"I, too, have heard this canard. It is without foundation; and even if it were, where is the crime? One can purchase it in any chemist's shop, diluted with grain alcohol and labeled laudanum; good for the miseries of the lumbago and all other manner of complaint. Had I been born to a caste lower than my own, I'd have hired a wagon and gone town to town peddling it by the quart."

A lawyer to the bone, *Monsieur* Bonaparte. A client is always innocent; but if guilty, then of nothing unlawful.

At length he squared away his stacks, palming the edges as even as bricks, and lifted one.

"Since, as I believe, you insist upon pressing forward despite my friendly advice, perhaps you will be so kind as to deliver these to your proposed victim."

Given the cordiality of the exchange so far, it seemed bad manners to leave him holding the bundle he offered. I turned it over, reading the delicate script on the top envelope. Like the rest, it was pressed from pale rose deckle-edged vellum, the whole bound with matching ribbon. It was addressed to "*O. Childress.*"

"They were sent by his fiancée in Virginia, an estimable woman by all accounts, and upon the evidence of her choice of husband, certainly. She has been waiting months for a reply."

"Childress has a fiancée?"

"Is it so strange a great man may love in the corporeal sense?"

"He hasn't been to Virginia in twenty years."

"The relationship is all the sweeter for the absence. Had the women I married respected my privacy to such an extent, I should not be alone this day."

I brought the bundle to my nose, but whatever scent she might have sprinkled on the envelopes had long since evaporated in that climate. "I'll do my best." I slid the letters into a side pocket.

"When you have finished reading them, please re-seal them as well as you can. He will not be fooled, but he will appreciate the gesture."

It was as bizarre a meeting as I'd attended, and I'd sat in on Indian tribal councils and armed truces during range wars in Wyoming. "Is that why you called me here, to tell me I'm a suicidal fool and ask me to deliver mail?"

"Not entirely." Felix Bonaparte returned the rest of the material to the folder and tied it securely. I wondered what it contained that he'd held back. "I doubt you welcome death, or you would not attend so to the weapon you carry. A man who ignores this precaution would ignore others, and not survive. The odds—odds; this is the word, *oui*?"

"A word, yes." His relentless courtesy had begun to stand my nerves on edge.

"Thank you; it's a hazard of my background and circumstances that I sometimes am not sure whether I am conversing in English, Spanish, or French. The *odds,* you must see, are decidedly in General Childress' favor. He would consider me small in the light of his own chivalrous nature if I did not attempt to bring them closer to even."

He pointed. He grew his nails long, but as round as coins.

"On that wall, *monsieur,* is a map more current than any you have seen. It was drawn by a German cartographer named Muehlig, who took it upon himself to chart all the impenetrable regions of the earth, and thus leave his footprint on the path of the great explorers. The dream ended when he was beheaded by *banditti* for the value of the surveying equipment he packed upon his burro; but not before he drew this. The *rurales* who apprehended and shot the brigands found it of no value compared to the other items they confiscated, and so were generous enough to offer it to me. It is less than ten years old, and thus three hundred years more current than any you may have seen. I cannot part with it, but I suggest you commit as much as you can of it to memory. It may mean your life—for a while.

"At the very least you will go to your grave knowing a bit more of where your bones will rest until trumpet's blow. To die is one thing, but to die lost—" Again he shrugged.

The map, framed in black walnut without glass, hung in gloom. I lifted the milk-glass shade off the nearest lamp and carried it over. The names of various peaks and canyons were in German; I ignored them, not because they were foreign but because they'd been named by men, and of no use to the man who roamed among them. Muehlig, using the inks and paints he'd carried, had washed the whole of the eastern coast of the Gulf of California in pale blue, but tinted the jagged bumpy region of the Sierra Madre a bilious shade that in the flickering flame inside the soot-smeared glass chimney seemed to throb, as if it had a pulse of its own, sickly green, like the discharge from an infected wound.

"The Mother Mountains, *monsieur,*" said the lawyer. "There the bones of the *Conquistadores* lay mingled with those of their predecessors, whose civilizations have been forgotten by time, buried by the very riches they sought. They died wealthy. If you will be so kind as to give me the name and address of your closest relation, I shall do my best to report where you were last seen alive."

I turned his way, and made as much of a bow as I could. It wasn't a patch on his, but he seemed to appreciate the effort. My last image of Felix Bonaparte, Esq., was of an arrangement of patches of light on a stoic face hovering above the lamp on his desk. If it weren't for the bundle of letters in my pocket, I'd have thought I'd dreamt the whole thing.

I passed back up the narrow alley, groping my way along the walls, which seemed closer together now, then farther apart, a vast expanse; I couldn't see as far as the one opposite. The adobe was hot to the touch. I snatched my palm away. I wondered if a fire was gutting the building. The heat followed me, coursed up my arm, across my chest, and down the other arm, passing out the ends of my fingers like electrical current. Raw cold rushed in to fill the void. I shivered. By the time I emerged from those thousand yards of darkness I was staggering.

The *Ghost* stood on its siding, inhaling flame and exhaling steam, its headlamp plowing a pale shaft through vapors as thick as churned butter. Hector Cansado, ghostlike himself, stood with his back to it, a moderate wind fluttering the end of the bandanna tied around his neck. He had the shotgun clamped to his right hip with the muzzle pointed at me.

I spread my hands. "It's Murdock."

"I know this." He didn't lower the weapon. "Stop walking, and keep your hands as they are."

I stopped. Of a sudden I felt no chills, no fever.

"I wondered how long it would take you to come around to that," I said.

"It requires no genius. There is the train, and here is the man who knows how to run it. Where, *Senor* Deputy, does that leave you?"

His image swam, shifted right and left, refusing to stay in one spot. I thought it was a distortion caused by the steam. I jerked my right arm, sliding the Bulldog revolver out of my sleeve into my hand. I leveled it and fired.

Missed.

I actually saw the slug float past him, riding the steam like flotsam on the ocean. I saw nothing after that but steam. It thickened, drifted around me, clung to my body, filled my eyes and nose, stung my nostrils. I was drowning in it. I clawed for the surface, lost my grip on the little belly gun. An hour passed before I heard it strike earth with a dull thump, as remote as at the bottom of a well two hundred feet deep.

By then I was falling, too, plummeting through the chill air of the well. I heard the roar of the shotgun, dull also, as if it were swaddled in the same steam that pulled me down and down and shut out the rest of my senses.

TWELVE

I was adrift on a calm ocean, jammed into a tight berth with the sun nailed to the sky like a cartwheel dollar, blinding me with its brilliance and draining all the moisture from my body, drying me out like a dead fly on a sill. The surface of the water was as flat as a sheet of iron. Then a great toboggan-shaped bank of blue-black cloud slid across my vision, blanking out the light and drenching me in icy cold. The wind came up, turning the surface of the ocean on end, the ship sliding down one wave and climbing another, dizzying me so I couldn't tell up from down. I gripped the edges of my berth so tightly I knew my fingers would never come unclamped; when the inevitable came, someone would have to break them to get me loose to throw over the side.

An angel came for me, or rather tried to reach me, but it never got close enough so that I could make out its features. All I saw was a white blur, always the same distance away, a bright star obscured by haze. That was the sum total of my life: help on the horizon, always just beyond arm's length.

Where there are angels, devils can't be far behind. Mine looked like Hector Cansado. His face was as big as the *Ghost*'s boiler, each of his nostrils like the bore of the Springfield shotgun whose stock he had braced against his shoulder, taking aim at me. Time and again I saw smoke erupting from the muzzle, the lead pellets coming my way, spreading as they went, the pattern the size of the mortar-and-timber wall of the building where Felix Bonaparte practiced law on behalf of Oscar Childress. When they struck, with the force of ten locomotives, I jerked out of my nightmare with a tongueless shout, but not into reality, only into another dream as bad. Every fugitive I had ever killed ran hot on my heels, Lefty Dugan foremost, bent double as he closed the distance so that I could see clear down inside the hole I'd bored in his head, the sides sleek and shining like the piston rods that propelled the train.

Then something broke, and I lay in a pool of cold sweat, my vision clear. I stared at the convex coffered ceiling of the parlor car, secure in the berth that folded up into the wall when it wasn't in use. I was alert, but weak to the point of death; when Joseph pulled me by my arms into a sitting position, then laid me back down to lift my legs, stripping away the sodden sheet, and repeated the process in reverse to replace it with fresh linen, I was as limp as a marionette in a medicine show. He had to raise my arms and brace them with one shoulder to change my nightshirt.

I slept then, without dreaming, or with no memory later of what I had dreamt, beyond the blazing coin nailed to the sky and the engineer and his shotgun and the icy rise and fall of the ship tossed by the sea.

"He can speak?"

A new voice, this, resonant, not loud, like the echo of cannonfire in the ears after a period of constant bombardment: a low rumble with a distinct Spanish accent.

"I am not a doctor, *Jefe.* The danger is past. I can say no more."

This voice was familiar. Joseph, the fireman I'd been too smart to trust; the one who'd saved my life, possibly twice. With Cansado gone to the other side there was none else to have gotten me into bed and seen me through the fever.

I raised my head, and thought at first I'd slipped back into delusion: The star burning brightly through haze was back, but with a difference. This time it managed to approach me, and as it drew near the blurred outlines became distinct, so that when it stopped at the edge of the berth and looked down at me I saw it was a man.

He was dressed in white, but not the shapeless dress of a peon; more like the sugar-cane barons one saw smoking cigars and reading newspapers in the lobby of the best hotel in El Paso, in a pressed linen suit and narrow-brimmed straw hat, squared across straight strong brows. The white was interrupted only by tobacco-brown skin, a parti-colored hatband, a thin black knitted necktie, and highly polished black boots, as small as a boy's. Everything about him, in fact, was small, but he was built perfectly to scale, so that you didn't realize he was anything less than normal stature until you had something to compare him to; in this case one of the overstuffed chairs, the nearest arm of which reached above his waist. I knew, had we stood face-to-face, he wouldn't tip back his head to look up, forcing me to tip mine forward if I wanted to meet his gaze. I would want to, rather than guess where he might be looking if not at me. To this day when I think of him I don't see him as small; and I do think of him.

He wore no emblem of office, and no weapon as far as I could tell. The suit was cut so carefully to his measure it didn't seem as if a pistol or knife could be concealed on his person. He introduced himself as Vigía Férreo, "Chief of police on approval."

I tried to wet my lips, but my tongue was as dry as a dead leaf. "On whose approval?" It came out in a croak. Immediately Joseph placed a hand against the back of my head, supporting it as he trickled water into my mouth from a gourd. Most of it splashed down my chin, but it tasted cool and mossy, as if it had been cranked up from the same deep well I'd fallen into when Cansado had leveled the shotgun at me. It seemed a hundred years ago. I wondered what had happened to him.

"The citizens of Alamos have granted me the honor. My predecessor was appointed by *El Presidente* Diaz. He died last month, and the city fathers are awaiting word from Mexico City regarding his replacement; but *los bandidos, senor,* they await nothing."

"Were you his deputy?"

"His mathematics tutor. He hoped for an accounting position in the state house in Hermosilla, but our merciful Lord had other plans for him." He crossed himself.

"Since when is long division a requirement for law enforcement?"

"None that I am aware of; but I was the only one he trusted with the key to the office, and the city fathers respected his judgment."

"What did he die of?"

"Yellow fever. It stalks this place like an old puma. You are the very first person I have spoken to who survived it."

"I've had practice in survival."

"So it would seem. Whom shall we bill for your engineer's burial?"

Now I knew the report I'd heard was the shotgun going off in some harmless direction, diverted by Joseph with whatever weapon he'd had at hand. "You might try *El Presidente,* who loaned the train and its crew to the federal seat in Montana Territory. Failing that, try Judge Harlan A. Blackthorne in Helena."

Férreo wrote the information on a starched cuff with a short stub of orange pencil. He seemed to make use of the same half-breed Chinese laundress as Bonaparte. I asked how the engineer had met his end.

"At the head of an axe."

I glanced at Joseph, whose face registered nothing. The fireman would be an artist with that tool.

Férreo seemed to have read my thoughts. "Our little village has witnessed much that it would perhaps be best to forget—it is, you see, the path of revolution and raids across the border—but I have never before seen a man cloven from the crown of his head to his waist. This man"—his eyes slid briefly to Joseph—"has provided me with an account of what took place three days ago. I should like to hear yours."

Three days? I thought it had been three hours. "He threatened me with a shotgun. That's the last thing I remember. If Joseph told you he killed Cansado in my defense, I'd take him at his word."

"I fear the word of an Indian does not travel as far as that of a white man."

"Then that's what happened. I'll sign an affidavit if you want."

"We are not so formal here. Can you enlighten me as to *Senor* Cansado's motives?"

"I can only think that he wanted to take over the train and sell it in the Sierras, along with his services as operator."

"*Senor* Bonaparte has informed me of your meeting in his office. You are still determined to press on with your mission?"

"I don't see how I can do that without an engineer."

"Nor without a train. In the name of the citizens of Alamos I am taking possession of it until further notice."

"What gives you that authority?"

He smiled, teeth blue-white against brown skin. "You may have three more days to regain your strength. Then you must make arrangements for other shelter or to return home. I shall hold the train until Mexico City sends someone to claim it.

"We live in a wilderness, *Americano*; wilder than anything in your frontier. A *bandido* with such transport as this is a dangerous animal. Moreover, to do other than I have chosen would be to countenance an act of murder. I do not believe that my predecessor would have done otherwise." He touched his hat. "*Buenos dias, Senor* Deputy. If you require anything that will make your stay more pleasant, please feel free to send me a message by way of the guards. The men I trust with such duty fought alongside Juarez. Juanito will be only too happy to show you his collection of gold teeth. You have but to ask."

After he left, I signaled to Joseph for another drink. The water tasted better than Blackthorne's Scotch whisky. I drank greedily, and would have gone on if he hadn't snatched the gourd away. "Why?"

"Lest you founder, like a horse."

"Not that. Why'd you take my side against Cansado?"

He lifted his shoulders and let them fall. "Perhaps I wished to be an engineer."

"You know how to run this train?"

"Stoking the fire is not the distraction you might think. I have had much time to watch and to remember what I have seen. All I need is someone to tend the boiler." A sly look crossed his hacked-out features. "I am afraid your days of riding in ease are at an end."

"Don't apologize. I was getting soft." I swung my feet to the floor. My head struck an invisible wall. I settled back onto the mattress. "I'd better rest," I said, when the car stopped spinning. "Stealing a train is a two-man job."

THIRTEEN

If I'd harbored any hope that the guards Férreo stationed to watch the *Ghost* were local amateurs pressed into service, it washed away when I alighted and saw them, one in front, one in the rear, and one on either side of the coach: slit-eyed Yaqui half-breeds with brown gnurled faces, carrying Mexican Winchesters at parade rest, bone-handled pistols in holsters with the flaps cut off attached to Sam Browne belts, short-bladed machetes balancing them out on the other side. A series of civil wars had provided them with surplus uniforms: riding breeches, knee-high boots and epaulets. They held their heads at the same ten-degree tilt to keep the smoke of their smoldering cheroots from collecting under the brims of their sombreros. They might all have been related, which was more than just a possibility: There were villages throughout that peninsula whose populations had bred among themselves for centuries, normally a recipe for weakness, but not in this case. Each generation appeared to have doubled the hardness of the last, like lichens forming additional inches to shelves growing on rock.

"Veterans of the revolution." Joseph spat and rubbed his spittle into the rug at his feet. "Bandits. *Tio* Benito could hardly pick and choose when killers were required." I couldn't tell if the avuncular reference to Juarez was genuine or marinated in sarcasm.

"My horse needs exercise." I shook my head when he stirred himself. "As do I."

He noted the wobble when I rose from the chair where I'd been resting, excused himself, and returned to the car a moment later carrying a crooked stick. "I was told to tap the wheels with it whenever we stop."

"Why?"

"*Quien sabe?* Cansado I think did not know either."

I took the stick. "What was the tribal remedy you treated me with?"

"The powder of the cinchona bark. This area is rich in the tree."

"I did you a disservice. Cansado said I couldn't trust you and I believed him."

"I trusted neither of you until he showed his hand. I am Aztec, after all, born with the earned wisdom of those who passed before. One traitor is to be expected. Two, they—" He faltered, made a gesture with his fists together, the thumbs turned away from each other.

"Cancel each other out."

"*Sí.* A double betrayal leads to faith."

The statement made as much sense to me as that entire business. I never did trust him entirely. It was like taking up with the woman who'd thrown one man over to take up with you.

The guards stood motionless, their eyes alone following me as I led the bay by its bit, as long as my steps took me no closer to the locomotive. Neither Joseph nor I was a prisoner, but their orders would be to prevent us from moving the train at any cost. Pressure was up; the fireman had seen to that while he nursed me, but every moment he stayed away from the tender was a loss of steam. Soon, keeping the train where it was would be no more than a formality. Without fire and water it was so much dead metal.

I walked alongside the tracks toward the caboose, then back, as much to restore strength to my muscles as to stretch the horse's sinews, supporting myself on the stick. Just for diversion I tapped a couple of wheels with the end, but if there was a crack in one it didn't sing out. In time that stick came to sum up the whole of my use to the federal court in Montana Territory. Judge Blackthorne abhorred the thought of any of his pistoleers lying idle. If not a Childress, then something else would have had to be trumped up to justify my time. The whole Mexican affair was nothing more than tapping a stick against an endless succession of wheels.

"Why not?" I said aloud.

"*Senor?*" The guard nearest me sent a blank expression my way.

"When was the last time you ate?" I asked.

"*Que?*"

I made a scooping motion toward my mouth. He shrugged. In all the years since I left Mexico I've never tried to imitate that gesture. Mexicans alone are educated in communicating through body movements; the roll of a shoulder, the lifting of an eyebrow, can out-debate William Jennings Bryan in the full cry of his eloquence.

I jerked my chin toward the parlor car. Not a muscle moved

in his face, but after a glance forward and back he took a step that direction. I hung back to let him board first, but he planted his boots in the cinderbed and motioned with his carbine's barrel. I mounted the steps and turned to clear the doorway. He had one foot on the plush rug when something moved in a swift blur. There was a thump and the guard teetered backward, falling away from his sombrero. Moving from instinct I caught him before he fell outside the train, swiveled my hips, and let him slide to the floor, snatching hold of the Winchester on the way.

Joseph stood on the other side of the open door, still holding the Springfield shotgun, butt foremost. The curtains across from me were drawn, blocking the view from the guard posted on that side. The Indian read my expression.

"This was your intention, no?"

"I was going to get him drunk, but I guess this is faster. What now?"

"I at least thought beyond the moment. The man who stands at the front of the train has a bladder the size of a *cucaracha*'s, but has trouble emptying it. He steps to the side every ten minutes and spends five minutes in the effort."

"How do you know?"

He reversed ends on the shotgun. My tin shaving mirror was lashed to the barrel with a bootlace. "I thought it best not to lean out the window."

"When did he make the trip last?"

"I cannot say. I was involved in waiting for this man." He gave him a stiff kick in the ribs. The guard grunted without stirring.

I used our prisoner's machete to cut the plush rope attached to one of the curtains and thrust it at him along with the crooked stick. "Tie him up and make sure he doesn't sing out."

He gave me the shotgun and looked wistfully at the Winchester, but I shook my head and leaned it in a corner. "I said keep him quiet, not silence him forever." He accepted the stick with a sigh. The window nearest the front of the car on the left was open. I poked the barrel outside, turning it until the guard near the locomotive was visible in the mirror. He yawned once, patting his mouth with the back of a hand; apart from that he was as immobile as a carved chief in a tobacco shop.

"Ten minutes, you said?"

A shoulder moved. His eyes remained on the man tied up at his feet, holding the stick in both hands poised to swing. "*Poco más o menos.* I do not own a watch."

"He seems to have cured himself since the last time. How long will that head of steam last?"

"Not long. I stoked the fire as hot as the gauge would stand to give me time to tend to you—as much and then some—but each moment lost—"

"Are you always this cheerful?"

He uncased two rows of tobacco-stained teeth in a ghastly grin.

The air was stifling; in that climate an open window brings no respite from the heat. The shotgun grew slippery in my grasp. I wiped one palm on my shirt, then the other. Steam drifting from the boiler condensed on the mirror in droplets that evaporated one by one before my eyes, and with them the life's-blood that kept the locomotive alive. The man in the glass showed no more life than an image in a tintype. The man on the floor groaned again; clothing rustled as Joseph prepared to silence him with the stick. I was about to put down his report as a beggar's wish when something rippled beneath the parched flesh of the man's face, a distinct surge of discomfort. He lowered his weapon and slid out of the mirror's range, walking rapidly with his toes turned inward, pigeon-fashion.

"Go!" I swept the mirror to the floor and traded the shotgun for the crooked stick. In a flash the Indian was out the door, feet crunching through the cinderbed as he made a dash for the engine.

Everything was against it, least of all the guard at the rear of the train stepping out far enough to see one of his charges making for the front. One well-placed shot and I'd be that most useless of creatures, a man with a contraption he didn't know how to run. Try selling that to a man like Harlan A. Blackthorne.

The guard he'd struck opened his eyes, saw me standing over him, and dropped his jaw to cry out. I swung the stick, catching him along the temple. His eyes rolled over white and his head fell back to the floor.

In the next moment I nearly fell myself. The floor lurched forward, my ankles turned, and I flung my shoulder hard against the wall, dropping my stick. Then as the train continued to pull, the floor slid the other way, resisting the pull of the hitch, but by then I had a grip on the frame of the door Joseph had left open and kept my footing. I snatched my hand away just as the door swung shut, sparing my fingers. The boiler chuffed steam, a live cinder from the stack flew through the open window, sizzling when it landed on a rug. I stepped over to crush it out with the toe of a boot, then went back to grasp the senseless guard by the collar, swing the door back open, and heave him outside before we reached lethal speed. At that he struck on his hip and shoulder and rolled three times.

As I pulled the door shut, something split the air by my left ear and knocked a piece out of the mahogany molding near the ceiling in the far corner, exposing raw yellow wood. I heard the report a quarter-second later, a shallow pop in the open air. Another slug starred a window, but had been fired at too shallow an angle to penetrate the glass. Through another window I saw Vigía Férreo running our way from the direction of town. He stopped, watching the train pick up speed. The face under the neat straw hat showed no emotion. The mathematics tutor–turned-policeman might have been calculating our rate of travel.

There was a thud overhead. I followed the sound to the window Joseph had left open, but laid aside the shotgun in favor of the machete I'd confiscated from the guard he'd struck. I waited with it raised, staring at the opening.

It took a week for a bone-handled Colt to come through it, clenched in the brown corded hand belonging to the man on the roof. I curled both hands around the machete's handle, hesitated to make sure of my grip, and swung it down with the force of an axe. Something hot splashed my cheek. Someone screamed hoarsely. The revolver, still attached to the hand, fell to the floor and slid across it, spraying blood from the stump of the wrist. The trigger finger tensed. The report was deafening in the enclosed space, but the bullet plowed a harmless path across the rug, burrowing like a mole. A moment later something flashed past the window: the rest of the guard I'd crippled, falling to the earth.

The adobe buildings sped past in a brown swipe. Just then the whistle brayed: a long and a short, followed by two longs, an impudent farewell. I thought that unnecessary. Adding train robbery to my employment history seemed enough without Joseph rubbing salt into an open wound. We were manufacturing enemies the way they cranked out machine parts in Chicago, and we hadn't even begun the climb into the Sierras.

FOURTEEN

A **dead hand** would make a fierce opponent at arm-wrestling. Luckily for me, this one came without an arm.

I pried the Colt loose, picked the hand and wrist up by the fingers, and pitched it out the window to rejoin its master in whatever afterlife awaited him. The fingers were warm and a little moist. They opened as it fell, like a crumple of paper losing tension or a supplicant asking for mercy.

I see that hand in dreams. At times it pleads, at others beckons. If the damned thing would just strum a guitar, or play a few bars of "Old Dan Tucker" on the piano, I might be rid of it; but it refuses to erase itself by becoming ludicrous.

I thought about packing the Colt along when I left the coach, but like the Winchester it was a Mexican copy of an American original made with inferior parts and unreliable, so I left them there and balanced myself out with the Deane-Adams and Bulldog revolver. The shotgun was too unwieldy and might pitch me to my death, so I left it as well and stepped out onto the car's verandah.

A steel ladder bolted to the back of the tender led to the top, but it was open, filled as recently as our stop in Alamos, rounded over with uneven chunks of mossy-smelling wood, and offered shifting and treacherous footing aboard a moving train. I climbed halfway up, gripped the top with both hands, and made my way around the corner, scrabbling with my feet until they found tenuous purchase on a nearly nonexistent ledge.

The *Ghost* was approaching forty miles an hour, but from where I stood it might have been going a hundred. Hatless, in my shirtsleeves, I clung to the tender, the hot wind buffeting my ears and snapping the ends of the bandanna around my neck. Given the choice I'd have turned around and gone back to the safety of the coach, but a train needs a fireman and the man assigned to that post was busy operating the locomotive.

Inch by inch, my fingers growing numb from the desperate tightness of their grip, I crept forward. I glanced down once, when my boot slipped, and saw the land dropping off nearly vertical to the piles of rocks at a base that seemed a mile below; and these were only the foothills. The mountains themselves shot straight up on the other side of the car, their peaks piercing the clouds like the tines of a fork.

I wasn't so much afraid of losing my grip as I was of surrendering it. In a flash—as if the train had turned a corner square into the sun—burning Mexico became frozen Nebraska, five years ago. I'd been either collecting or dropping off a prisoner, in a city I've forgotten the name of, when the clanging of the bell belonging to the pump-wagon, the town's pride and joy, brought my attention to the half-finished steeple of the Methodist church, where a carpenter clung to the remnants of a scaffold that had collapsed beneath him. The ladder just reached him, but as the volunteer stretched to take his hands, the carpenter let go, plummeting without a cry to the street below. He didn't die immediately, but lingered on, succumbing to pneumonia on his third day on the cot in the doctor's back room. My business was finished, but I stayed on to hear the end of the story. The Methodist pastor declared his passing the work of Satan during his services, but in his quarters later told me that Death was a siren, whose call was sometimes more strident than the will to live. At the thought, I felt the backs of my knees tingle with the thrill of instant release. That made me tighten my hold. I would not be ruled by my joints.

I was nearly to the cab when we swung around a bend, the train seeming to lean out from the shelter of the hill forty-five degrees. My feet swung clear; I was like a shirt on a clothesline blown out straight by a gust of wind. An image flashed into my mind, a photograph I'd seen in a book, of a train lying full on its side, the hollow V-shaped underside of the cowcatcher exposed like the tender flesh under a man's chin.

I lost my grip, scrabbled wildly at the smooth side of the tender, but some infernal force had pulled the edge of the top beyond my reach; the car seemed to have increased in height. Groping in panic, I came to a rod of some kind mounted horizontally, and threw my other hand up beside the first just as the train entered a bend in the opposite direction. I didn't know the rod's purpose; probably not to encourage some reckless fool to suspend himself from it. For what seemed an hour I hung loose as a broken shutter, my legs dangling free two hundred feet above an earth made entirely of broken stones like eggs hatched by some extinct bird. I hung that way, arms dead to the shoulders, until we straightened out. A toe found the ledge. I groped with my other foot, placed it beside the first, spread my legs, braced myself, released and flexed each hand in turn until circulation came tingling back, grasped the rod again, bounced on my knees three times, counting, and hurled myself forward through the opening at the rear of the cab.

For a third of a second I was airborne, prey to the first crosswind that would hurl me out the side into open air. Then I landed, throwing myself sideways to avoid colliding with Joseph, standing at the front with a hand on the throttle. I came up shoulder-first against something diabolically hard sticking out of the cab's side, bruising the bone and turning my lungs inside out. I feel the tender spot still when the barometer drops; and it's been forty years since I rode outside a train.

The man at the throttle glanced back over his own shoulder. "I gave you up."

"You almost did on that last bend." I rubbed the place where I'd struck, gasping for breath.

"I dared not stop. These hills swarm with bandits who fall upon everything standing still and worry it to the bone."

I nodded. That last effort had exhausted the wind I needed for conversation.

He pointed at the firebox and a pair of sooty leather gloves jammed inside the handle. "We are losing steam."

I nodded again, put on the gloves, and fell upon the woodpile. I wrenched free a squarish chunk, opened the box, and poked the wood inside. It caught like a curl of paper, the flames burning blue along the bottom edge. I repeated the action until there was no more room in the box. The heat drew all the moisture from my pores and baked my face until I was sure it was as dark as the Indian's.

"Take the wood from the bottom. The rest is green."

I was no longer *senor* to him. His promotion to master of the *Ghost* hadn't come so suddenly he'd failed to note the shift in our relationship.

From Alamos we climbed and climbed, the scenery turning from green to near black in its density; my ears popped, and still we were only in the foothills. To our left the country rose in succeeding folds of old-growth wood, the limbs pregnant with leaves, the trunks straight up and down and as close together as ribs of corduroy. They had no place to fall if they fell. It seemed nothing could squeeze between them: yet when I wasn't stoking the fire Joseph kept me entertained with stories of marauding bears, half-human predators, and pumas that pounced without warning.

"We have them up north," I said.

"Not like these cats. They strike with the sun at their backs, making no noise, so that you are aware of one only when it is eating you alive."

"You've seen this?"

"Eben, my sister's husband, died in this way. I could do nothing; so of course I watched."

His family, it turned out, was a wealth of uncles, cousins, and brothers-in-law whose deaths he'd witnessed, or whose remains had been found half-devoured after days of searching. To hear him tell it the local wildlife had been living on the sole diet of his people for generations. I couldn't tell how much of what he said was truth and how much invention, to keep me under his influence; but I found the heft of the two revolvers reassuring.

As I chucked wood, I couldn't stop thinking about the pistol Hector Cansado had told me he had hidden somewhere in the cab, the one he claimed Joseph didn't know existed. Just because the Indian had saved my life didn't mean he wouldn't reclaim it the moment I was no longer needed, and there was no sense in allowing him a weapon beyond the axe he'd used on the engineer. DeBeauclair, the vanished Pinkerton, had reported Oscar Childress' recruitment of Indians into his private army. The promise of plunder would explain why Joseph had chosen to press on rather than turn back.

Every time I pulled something out of the tender I expected the fabled pistol to fall out. There didn't seem to be any other place in those close quarters, crowded as they were with levers, gauges, handles, and every description of cast-iron protuberances, to have concealed it, and I had to be ready to scoop it up when it appeared.

Unless he'd found it already and had it hidden under his overalls.

Up and up we scaled into the black heart of the Mother Mountains, the engine laboring like a broken-winded mount, guided only by a map whose artists were dust and the memory of a fleeting glimpse at the updated chart in Felix Bonaparte's office, with its bilious green blob representing what Blackthorne had called the ideal habitat of dragons.

Thought of the attorney in his modern circumstances brought me back from the medieval nature of our present location.

"Where's the nearest telegraph office after Alamos?" I shouted above the straining of the engine.

"Cabo Falso. Four hundred miles."

"We can expect a welcoming party there. Férreo wouldn't have lost any time wiring the authorities we're on our way."

"There are no authorities in Cabo Falso. It is run by whores and brigands."

"That's a relief. I thought we might be in trouble."

Teeth showed in a face stained permanently by soot. Apart

from that, his having taken full possession of the controls, I found it hard to tell him from the slain engineer.

Higher yet, and then we leveled off, chugging along the brawny shoulder of the mountains. The sun blazed red briefly, flickering like wildfire between passing trunks, then vanished, as if snuffed out between a monstrous thumb and forefinger. In the sudden darkness, pairs of eyes glittered green in the reflected light of the lamp mounted on the front of the boiler, like cold jewels strung out raggedly. Absent the pull of gravity, I found time between replacing logs to ask if there was a place where we might put up for the night. I wasn't up to full strength yet, and the trip alongside a speeding train had been no remedy. My muscles burned from tugging loose logs and stooping to pitch them into the firebox. Belatedly, I realized that apart from the inevitable watery broth to keep up my constitution I hadn't eaten in days.

"In ten miles, perhaps," he said, "if there are no rockslides to stop us before then. Pray there are not. If the tracks are blocked, we must reverse directions for as many miles as we have traveled, and since this train does not move as fast backwards, what bandits we have passed would find it a simple thing to board us from above, when we are too busy with the engine to defend ourselves. We must not stop below these rotten shelves of shale." He pointed upward through the cab opening, to ragged escarpments of black against a sky only slightly less dark. Pallid starlight showed through semicircular spaces, like fresh bites taken from a crust of bread.

"Does this country never relent?"

"You have not yet seen her at her worst."

He said it with a kind of pride. Everyone has a proprietary interest in the place he calls home. In the absence of anything good to boast of, he'll compete with anyone for the bad.

He wasn't exaggerating, as it turned out. I once survived three days and two nights in a barn stacked with frozen corpses in the comfort of knowing that at least it wasn't the Sierras.

For a long time we traveled in silence. Then he said:

"There is a dugout, carved into the rock by no one knows who, no one knows how long ago, with logs for shelter from monsoons; the originals have rotted away, but those who come there to rest have replaced them from time to time. It has been used by trappers, missionaries, and other wanderers. If it is still there it would be a safe place to spend the night. Such rocks as might fall have fallen already, and one can see all the way to the valley below."

"What about above?"

He tugged on the whistle. A bull elk that had been preparing to cross the tracks swung its great antlered head our way, eyes glowing in the light of the lamp, and backed away into the woods.

"If you seek to be safe from everything, you should never have come to this place."

FIFTEEN

At first I thought the dugout had fallen in, or been carried away by rocks; the Sierras were continually shifting shape, like the beasts in Indian lore. The spot Joseph had pointed out, cleared from forest that had grown right up to the tracks, looked swept clean in the shaft of light from the champing locomotive: A crumb-scraper couldn't have been more thorough. Then the fog and drifting steam parted to expose something black and gaping, as if the mountain had opened its mouth to expel sulphurous smoke from its lungs. It was the entrance to a structure erected in partnership between nature and man.

Joseph busied himself with the engine while I retrieved the Whitney rifle and scouted out the location, gripping the weapon in one hand and a bull's-eye lantern in the other. I tipped open the louvers, directing the beam inside the arrangement of mossy logs with a roof made of rocky outcrop and an extension of poles shingled with bark. Apart from the usual rubbish of temporary habitation and the palpable odor of earth, mildew, and sodden wood-ash, it was unoccupied, at least by humans. I'd half expected to disturb a sow bear sleeping with her cubs or at the very least a nest of rats. A beetle nearly the size of my hand stirred and scaled the Pike's Peak of my toe, that was all. I shook free of it and hung the lantern from the end of a pole by its bail to investigate the rest.

A pile of moldy rags got the attention first of my nose, then my eyes as a likely resting place for rattlers. It lay heaped in the corner where a windscreen of logs chinked with clay and dead leaves met the side of the hill, where a previous tenant would have flung it to lighten his load before venturing back out. I picked up a stick, poked at the heap, and when nothing issued forth twisted the stick, winding a bit of rotting cloth around the end, and tugged it free. Something tumbled out, rattling like hollow wooden flutes; something rolled across the packed clay floor and came to rest against my foot, leering up at me with the porcelain grin of death.

I started; but I'd seen human skulls before. Stripped of flesh and gutted of brains, they offered no harm. It wore a patch of black hair like peat on a rock and two inches above the right eye-socket a hexagonal hole as big as my fist. It might have been made by a stone falling, but I doubted it.

"*Que pasa?*" Joseph's call, bent out of shape by damp and distance. I ignored it, stirring the stick among the bones. Something crackled; I speared it and brought it up into the light. It was a scrap of foolscap, as yellow as any of the dead leaves stuck among the chinking between the logs, but marked with script written in faded ink:

gone up the tracks for help, but

That was it: a journal entry of some kind. Who'd gone up the tracks for help I might never know, but if he'd returned with it he'd been too late.

I brought the scrap close to my eyes. It seemed to be deteriorating as I looked at it, from sudden exposure to the open air, like the mummified remains of an ancient Incan king disinterred after centuries; but it was more recent than that. Like Judge Blackthorne, I had little faith in a man's personality revealing itself in his hand, but I knew a closed loop from an uncrossed *t*; and I knew as sure as I was a hundred miles from the civilized world that I was reading the last words of Agent DeBeauclair, the Pinkerton operative who'd disappeared after filing his last report on Oscar Childress.

"A friend?"

I jumped again. Joseph stood in the entrance, the light from the lantern lying on his square cheeks and the edge of the axe in his hand.

"DeBeauclair is a French name, *sí*?" The Indian crunched cracked corn. "I would think he would look more foreign."

I sat across the fire from him in the entrance of the dugout, the Whitney across my lap. The fire was of my own making, chunks from the tender chopped into kindling with the axe Joseph had brought. The light of the flames crawled and twitched over the bone face where it had come to rest, changing its expression from amused idiocy to deep contemplation. Outside, tree frogs, night birds, crickets, and cicadas made a racket, as deafening as in any city. The bay, hobbled just outside the halo of heat, grazed and switched its tail at mosquitoes the size of chimney swifts. I ate beef from the tin with a spoon, washed it down with water, and passed him the canteen. "We're all the same under the skin. What do you think made that hole?"

"A rock from a sling or a stone axe." He drank, his jaws grinding without cease. His molars must have been worn down to stumps.

"Not a ball from a percussion weapon."

"I know of none that would make a wound that size."

"I do. I saw my share of them in the war."

"I cannot think why white people should make war on each other except over horses."

"We can't all be as civilized as Indians. Who do you think he sent for help?"

"Someone unreliable, I should think."

Something cried, sounding close. In town, I would have put it down to a colicky baby. In that country it made the hairs bristle at the top of my spine. "There's your puma. You must have a cousin or two left."

"I think I am that cousin. Perhaps my great-great-grandfather destroyed all the litter-mates of a cat that has sworn not to die until it has done for his family as well."

"It didn't kill the detective, that's plain. There'd be no bones left to tell the tale."

"Bandits. Yellow fever, and the hole came later. The great bird of death swooped down and snatched his soul. Where is the good in guessing? *He* is beyond caring."

"He cared enough to write something, but that scrap is all that's left." I'd found a ball of shredded paper left by a brood of mice. They'd built the nest inside the dead man's rib cage, from the record of his last days. "What was he doing here? It's a long way into the wilderness, even if he rode a horse or took along a pack animal."

He helped himself to another handful of corn. "What are *you* doing here?"

"They say, even his enemies, that Childress is a brilliant man. I came to see what makes him shine."

"You wish to learn from him about horses and making money?"

"If he brings them up; not that I care a shuck about horses, and money runs out between my fingers like water. I expect to hear about poetry, philosophy, history, governing, science, and religion."

"What will you do with what you learn?"

"Something, possibly. Nothing, maybe. Sometimes knowledge alone is enough."

He shook his head, rooting in his sack for corn. Those loose kernels had reality for him, purpose and meaning.

"And after you have learned these things, you will kill him."

"Those are the orders. The killing, that is. I added the other."

"It is like squeezing all the good out of an orange and throwing away the skin."

"Very like." I scraped up the last of the beef, ate it, and set the tin on the ground.

He turned his face into the wind. It carried the smell of brimstone. "The dry season is early. We must take on water tomorrow. There is a tower twenty miles ahead. Nearer twenty-five. After that we must draw it from the earth."

"A village?"

He shook his head. "Only the tower, and such as gathers there. Good local beer and a woman."

"Just one?"

"I would not say 'just' of this woman."

His face showed no amusement. A man of his kind, in

a place like that, didn't leer about such things. They were like water and meat. "What about you?" I asked. "What made you come all this way?"

He spoke without raising his eyes, poking a stick at the fire. They reflected the light like pieces of polished coal.

"I wish to be the first of my people to pilot a train from the top of Mexico to the bottom. Then perhaps I will be made an engineer in truth as well as in name."

"That's important?"

"My father and all my brothers died, either in the mines or from the dirt that filled their lungs. It is not my wish to die as they did."

"They should be grateful."

He looked up at me sharply, his hand still gripping the stick. "Why?"

"The mines got to them before the puma."

He looked down again and resumed stirring the ashes. "I did not think of that."

The noises from outside increased, as if whoever directed them had raised his baton. Further conversation seemed not worth the effort to compete. I mixed water from the canteen with a handful of Arbuckle's and set the pot on a flat rock by the fire, turning it from time to time as the Indian munched.

"Do you think the men who run the railroads will not want to make me an engineer because I killed the one I worked for?"

"Not the railroad men I've met."

He smiled, pieces of corn shell stuck between his teeth. When the coffee was ready I filled two cups and handed him one. He wrapped his hands around the tin as if they needed the heat, but he didn't drink from it at first. "I think they would choose the puma," he said.

"Who?"

"My father and my brothers. It is better to be eaten by an animal than by the dust from a shaft."

"Quicker, anyway."

Outside the dugout the big cat cried.

SIXTEEN

The hot wind blew perpendicular to the train, booming the side of the stock car where the bay doubtlessly fiddle-footed and tossed its head, trying to crawl out of its hide. My own skin prickled as if I'd fallen into a crock of needles. I was afraid to touch my lips in case they peeled off in paper-thin layers. Every time I stoked the fire I felt like a pig on a spit, my skin turning orange and crackling. Joseph, manning the throttle and leaning out the opening on his side to look ahead for obstructions, showed no reaction other than to take a long draught from the canteen when I handed it to him. A goatskin bag hung inside the cab, pregnant with water, but he told me to resist using it to refill the canteen. He didn't say why.

I looked out at the pinon and fescue flying past. The green seemed to fade as I watched, the grass blades shriveling like dead petals on a fireplace grate. "What about fires?" I asked.

"I brake as little as possible, but one cannot prevent every spark. The thing is to keep the burning country behind us."

"What happens when we stop?"

"Oh, the fires stop too. We have an agreement, this place and I."

They say, the experts back East who know everything, that Indians have no humor in the white man's understanding of the term. I've been the length and breadth of the West looking for one who could answer an honest question with anything but a macabre joke.

When we did stop, to conserve steam for the last run to the water tower, we struck off down the track to confirm his agreement with the wilderness. I carried six pails of sand, strung out three on each side of a yoke across my shoulders, which I used to put out sporadic buds of flame along the cinderbed while Joseph chopped brush with his faithful axe, piled it, and wet it down with water from the goatskin bag to create a firebreak.

"You might have told me what it was for." I tugged my bandanna back down below my chin. The top half of my face would be black.

"Too much talking dries the throat."

I watched the wind baking the wetness from the limbs. I could smell wood still burning a mile or so down the rails, hear the whoosh of flame consuming a parched pinon in one gulp. "I can't claim confidence."

"You expect too much. These forests have burned to the ground many times. They continue to burn until the rains come, or until they reach woods so dense the flames can find no more air to breathe. It has always been so, a thousand times a thousand years before men came with sand and water to put them out, or there would be no trees left to burn. To slow down the fire is as much victory as we can expect."

As we turned back toward the train, something rustled in the undergrowth; a deer or an elk, possibly a bear. The woods were too dense for my eyes to penetrate. I remembered the cry of the puma, and Joseph's constant reference to bandits, and picked up my pace. I'd left the Whitney rifle behind to carry the pails and didn't like the odds of defending myself with hip guns from an enemy I couldn't see. I wasn't sure I could even slow it down.

The *Ghost* labored up a long grade, panting like a stove-in horse. For an hour and a half Joseph had been staring at the gauges with an expression I never want to see on a doctor's face with me as the patient. I had the impression we were running on a teaspoon of water, and asked if what was left in the canteen, the goatskin, and the kegs of fresh drinking water in the parlor car would help.

"A drop in the ocean," he said. "We have fifty gallons in the boiler, and to expect it to take us beyond this grade would be to tempt God."

It was my first intimation that he'd been converted; and my first lesson in just how much even a small engine drank.

Nearing the top we slowed to a crawl. Less than that; it seemed the trees were moving forward rather than backward, and slowly enough at that to count the leaves. If any bandits were close at hand, that would be the time to strike. Over and over again I rehearsed in my mind the move toward the Whitney rifle leaning in the corner, wondering if I'd be better served by the shorter distance to one of the revolvers on my hips. The moment required for the decision alone, in the heat of action, might kill us both.

The boiler wheezed; the stack cried for smoke, I fed the box. The drive-rods that turned the wheels strained agonizingly slow, like a milk-maid churning at the edge of fatigue, rotating stubborn steel against the friction of the rails, steel also: What had been designed as a partnership of identical elements was deteriorating into a contest, Philadelphia versus Detroit, or more internally still, the fraction of temperature between one smelting-vat and another. The slightest variance in joints, a spike driven an eighth of an inch off true, or not driven flush, a tiny flaw in the crucible back at the finery, a bubble formed when a piece was removed from the cast; an indifferent laborer a thousand miles away at the end of his shift, who said good was good enough, and fair fair, had sealed the fates of two men in a place whose name on a map he couldn't pronounce.

What if it wasn't an illusion, and we were rolling back down the grade? Would the brakes hold, or would the natural law of gravity take over where the efforts of man had failed, plummeting us at breakneck speed toward the level, where a sharp curve I remembered would flip us off the rails like an annoying bug, the whole ludicrous link of cars like a string of sausages sent down the steep flanks of the Mother Range into a pile of scrap iron and crushed flesh at the base?

Was I raised in a trapper's shack at the top of the Bitterroots to die in a tangle of metal at the bottom of a pimple of a hill in Mexico?

"There it is," said Joseph.

I started. He'd said it as if we'd come through a light rain into bright sunshine.

It was bright, at that, shining on a squat wooden barrel the size of my furnished room in Helena, mounted on spindly legs of pine bound with thongs with the bark intact. Beads glittered on the staves as on a glass of ice-cold beer.

"I wondered some," he said. "She was working herself that last half-mile."

"'Wondered'?" I wanted to swallow back the word; I knew I'd been had for a fool.

He leaned on the brake, his face grave. "I always worry along this stretch. It asks much of a boiler this size."

It had been an initiation of some kind. I should have recognized it, army and bunkhouse veteran that I was. All that talk of pumas and bandits and relatives done to violent death had lured me into the oldest game of all. He was leaning out the opening on his side. I waited for him to turn away before I struck him between the eyes. I saw his shoulder stiffen; not at the thought of my assault, but by something he'd seen up ahead. By the time he drew himself back inside, my fist was back down at my side. I don't know now if it was his dead-blank expression that made me relax my fingers or the stench prickling the hairs in my nostrils. They'd become inured to the smell of burning, but this one came with the sweet tint of roast pork. I'd come across it before, not at communal events behind a ranch house, but in the heat of battle, with dead men shot at such close range the powder-flare set fire to their flesh.

He alighted; but not before tugging his bandanna up around his nose and mouth. I did the same with mine and stepped down behind him.

There was no smoke; the fires that had caused it had gone out long since. Beyond the water tower, which had remained untouched, a briarpatch of blackened timber poked up at random angles from acres of ash; knee-deep, should one want to wade into it. We didn't. The stench of burnt flesh alone held us back. Such shells of humanity that lay swaddled in those ashes would add nothing to what we already knew.

A white boulder, sunk so far into the earth as to suggest it had tumbled down from the mountains years before, bore a sign, etched likely with a charred stick and pounded pale gray by sporadic rainfall: a reverse crucifix, with the crosspiece at the bottom.

Joseph crossed himself, confirming my suspicions of conversion, and pronounced three syllables that chilled the oven-baked Sierras to the bone:

"Cholera."

I placed my palm against my bandanna, pressing it to my face. "Not yellow fever? You said there's plenty of cinchona in these woods."

"For that, they would not try to burn out the contagion and then flee. There is no medicine for this evil. It kills and kills until it has gorged itself with death."

"Do we turn back?"

He was silent; thinking. After a moment he shook his head.

"No. They have burned it out, the survivors. Their only hope to survive is to press ahead."

"And if they haven't burned it out?"

"Then they carry it with them; or turn back to escape it." He stared at the ground. "I was wrong. I think they have turned back. There is nothing ahead."

"What about the water?"

He was motionless; then shook himself and tilted his chin toward the squat tower.

"The *Ghost* is already dead. No contagion can infect it. We will fill up and move on."

"You're sure they turned back? That they haven't taken the disease into our path?"

Just then something whooshed, a half-mile down track, if that: another stand of trees gone up in flame.

"The fire behind," he said; "the plague ahead. What have we to lose?"

SEVENTEEN

With both hands, Joseph tugged an extra cap down to the bridge of my nose, pulled up my bandanna, and tied it tight around the lower half of my face, with all the firm and caring attention of a mother bundling up her child to go out into a blizzard.

"Shield your eyes with your sleeve when you twist off the top," he said. "We let the pressure drop, but the water's still hot enough to poach a steer."

I climbed the ladder to the boiler, pausing twice to rest; in spite of all the exercise stoking the firebox, I'd yet to retrieve all my strength. The spout attached to the water tower was at the end of my reach. I braced a foot against the brass grab-rail, hooked a hand under the roof of the cab, and leaned out almost perpendicular to the locomotive, snatching the spout by its chain and swiveling it into place. I wore the leather gloves, but wrapped a rag around my hands before I bent to the boiler's cap, which was about the size of the lid of a gallon jar of pickles and took twice as much effort to twist loose even with the aid of a wrench the size of a mule's hind leg. Once it gave enough to do the rest with one hand, I slung my other arm across my eyes, leaned back, and jerked loose the cap, releasing a geyser of white water and steam whose heat I felt through the bandanna, my borrowed overalls, heavy flannel shirt, and long-handles. When it died down I lowered the spout into the opening and tugged on the cable that lifted the gate. Water pulsed through the crimped-together steel tubes like blood through an artery.

Waiting for the boiler to fill, I took in the view. At my back rose the wall of wooded mountains, as black as the hills of Dakota, while in front of me the land sloped down to a green-and-brown shelf stretching for miles to the gulf, which I couldn't quite see but could determine its existence by an open expanse of sky with nothing to obscure it but white clouds that seemed to touch the shore. It seemed to me I could smell the salt water, but that was imagination; miles of desert would have absorbed all the moisture and replaced it with the odor of earth scorched by the sun. Down track I saw the way we'd come, and a smudge of smoke belonging to the still-smoldering fires ignited by sparks from the *Ghost*'s wheels. Up track, their smoke vanished sometime since, piles of ash pierced by gaunt charred timbers marked the graves of the men and women (I thought of Joseph's "I would not say 'just' of this woman") who had lost their fight with cholera. The cleansing flames had spread as far as the rails, but after strolling along them and back, the engineer had reported the steel intact.

"What about the ties?"

"Burned through, a few. We'll go slow and pray for the best."

Back on the ground, the box heating back up, the tender

filled with freshly chopped wood and the pressure rising, I gripped the Whitney rifle and scanned the forest for signs of bandits, but Joseph said the miasma of death would likely keep them away. "A clean bullet, or the jerk of a noose, these things hold no terrors for them. They did not take up the work to perish in a wallow of their own sweat and vomit."

I'd begun to wonder if his tales of land-bound pirates hadn't been glossed up a bit, like the stories of mountain lions stalking his family exclusively; but as we pulled forward I continued to divide my attention between the dense growth and the fire, with now the added detail of the burned ties.

We moved at walking pace, the wheels barely turning. As we approached the scorched acre of ground, my belly tightened, jerking itself into a knot when the floor lurched under my feet. Joseph didn't stop, but the long muscle in his jaw stood out like taut cable as he teased the throttle forward. Something crunched: the crushing of the weakened ties under the weight of the train. The earth shifted, like plates sliding; the rails, unsupported, splayed beneath the pressure of the wheels. My hands gripped the edge of the cab's opening and the handle of the brake lever on the other side, anticipating the drop when the wheels slid off the spreading rails. My bunched knuckles seemed to be fraying through the leather gloves. If the left gave way, we'd tilt toward the mountains, and be stranded without the equipment to set the wheels back onto the tracks. If the right, the train would yield to the pull of its own weight, tumbling down the steep hillside like a string of milk cans held together by cord, and us with it if we failed to jump clear. My hands were clamped so tight I couldn't imagine any power that would free them. I thought of some stranger months later coming upon my remains like Agent DeBeauclair's, the bony fingers still hanging on to the crushed cab as if welded.

Another lurch snapped my teeth together. The earth was dropping out from under us. The muscle in Joseph's jaw twitched—he couldn't have prevented it even if all his concentration weren't centered on maintaining pressure on the throttle—but apart from a hissing through his nose he made no sound. Gently he eased the control forward, as if he were urging a skittish horse across a swaying bridge. This drew a noise from the boiler like a sudden intake of breath and then a shorter stroke from the drive-rods that turned the wheels, with an accelerated *huh-huh-huh* from the pistons: The *Ghost* was giving birth.

The panting increased, we picked up speed. The broken ties were behind us.

I let out my breath, pried loose my fingers, and flexed blood back into them. I waited for a flippant remark from Joseph. None came; this time he'd been on the same edge with me.

We'd dodged one disaster, but the place we were in was lush with it.

A cluster of leaves hanging like bunched grapes at the end of a branch stirred sharply, with no such movement among its neighbors to suggest a gust of wind or the draw of the train passing. A bird, possibly, taking flight from its perch, or an elk browsing for fodder. But there was an unnatural abruptness in the motion, as of something invading from outside the wilderness. A week ago I'd have thought nothing of it. I'd developed a connection with all that dense growth almost as close as the one I'd formed with the train itself. It wasn't my first extended stay so far outside civilization, but there was something about the Sierras that was apart from all the untracked places I'd seen, as if they'd been dropped there by something flying from one world to another. If I'd been so deeply absorbed into them in so short a time, how much more difficult must it be to separate Oscar Childress from his place of exile?

The hot wind blew without ceasing, crackling in my ears, standing the hairs on the back of my hand at military attention, extending the nerves beneath the skin to the tips, so that the slightest change in its direction stung them like live sparks; and when it changed, it boomed like Lee's artillery at Cold Harbor. I blinked constantly, to lubricate my eyes; but they sizzled on the instant of drawing open the lids, like side-pork frying in an iron skillet. When the *Ghost* turned a bend into a fresh hot gust, it was as if the desert below had stood on end and smacked me in the face with all the dead dry weight of sand and desiccated skeletons and granite ground down to powder by the hot wind. I drank from the canteen, guzzled from the goatskin bag, and full upon the orgasm of water on my throat came the sensation that it had expelled itself the way it had come, in the form of pure steam; if I dared to exhale, it would come out as smoke. I felt my intestines roasting; I could almost smell them turning into tripe.

When I pushed my face into the slipstream outside the cab, in search of at least the illusion of cool air, I saw always in the next bend of the rails a pool of blue water. I didn't care if mermaids swam in it, or if it was alive with leeches; it was neither hot wind nor dry sand. Men had died crawling toward that illusion. I couldn't help but think that in the last moment before death they'd experienced something close to satisfaction.

They'd triumphed, in their way. What did it matter whether a man withered into the earth like a fallen leaf or rotted at the bottom of a six-foot grave, one with the pine boards that had contained him? The first fed the coyotes and carrion-birds, the second worms, gray slick creatures who laid eggs to make more worms. Birds flew, at least, crossing vast territories in moments, blinking down at trains crawling beneath them at forty miles an hour; coyotes hunted and mated and cried at the moon. It shone back. All it did for me was hang in the sky, drum its fingers, and wait for dawn. We were strangers who passed on the street.

It was the yellow fever talking. The moon was just a hole punched in the sky when you were in the pink of health.

Even as I bent to scoop yet another of the endless chunks of wood into the firebox—the next in line rolled into the former's place with all the inevitability of loose dirt filling a hole—I felt the amputated hand of the man I'd slung the axe at while leaving Alamos, caressing my burning muscles, forgiving in every stroke what I'd done to him and telling me it wasn't so bad on the other side, where all were made whole and the water ran blue and ice-cold, ideal for mixing with Judge Blackthorne's good Scotch whisky.

"To hell with that," I said aloud. "He cut it straight from the Missouri before he sent it aboard. I caught a minnow in my teeth."

"Something?"

Joseph, hand on the throttle as always, turned his graven-idol head thirty degrees in my direction.

I shook myself loose of everything not connected to the cab I was riding in. It was just that, after all: a construction of wood on an iron frame, propelled by fire and water through a landscape carved from common clay.

"Nothing. How far to civilization?"

"Civilization? A thousand miles. Two hundred to Cabo Falso; Cabo Infierno, if you prefer. We should be there by week's end."

Two hundred miles to Cape Hell. It seemed that I'd spent my entire life at that same point.

EIGHTEEN

Nothing changed. We might have been standing still while the trees rolled by on our left and the foothills fell behind on our right, propelled by some cranking mechanism of their own. Even the birds flying from one high branch to the next might have been jerked on invisible wires, their cries made by wooden blocks scraping against each other. The motion of the wheels and the swaying of the locomotive were the only stability I knew; if the train were to stop and I to alight from it, I'd walk with a rolling gait as if the earth itself were in motion, like a sailor cast ashore after months at sea. The *Ghost* was reality, solid ground the phantom. Nothing was unexpected; not even the lump of white-hot lead that sparked off the cab's frame, so close to my face I thought a match had been struck off the tip of my nose.

We'd slowed for a sharp curve, our bodies leaning instinctively toward the mountains, as if our combined weight would have any effect on the pressures pulling tons of iron out into space; whoever had fired the shot had been waiting for that, had probably picked the spot knowing we'd have to reduce speed to make the bend.

Joseph was first to react. He shouted something in a language I'll never know and hurled his upper body out the opening opposite the source of the bullet, placing as much steel between it and himself as he could within the cramped space we shared. I was more sluggish, lulled into a standing doze by the monotonous movement the way I'd slept in the saddle during long drives; but I came around after a beat, snatched up the Whitney rifle, and sent a slug flying into the dense growth. I had no target, only the desperate need to announce to whoever it was we were more than sitting fowl.

Hell came after.

I thought at first we'd hit a section of rough track and were rattling over a series of sharp joints. We were speeding up, trying to outrun the attack, and the chopping noise kept pace. Then a piece of the wooden post holding up the roof came apart and something stung my hand and when I looked at it blood was spreading from a ragged hole shorn through the leather. I'd been grazed by a sliver of iron from the firebox or a shard of shattered lead ricocheting off it. The broken edge of the roof looked as if it had been chewed up by a sawmill blade. A ribbon of shining chips was stitched across the stoveblack surface of the panel where the gauges were mounted; one of the thick glass lenses was starred.

I knew then I'd lost another piece of my innocence. As often as I'd been shot at, this was the first time I'd stood in front of a Gatling gun in operation.

I dove for the floor, snatching hold of Joseph's sleeve and jerking him down alongside me. His face registered surprise and rage, but when he looked down at the offending hand and the dark stuff that was staining his sleeve, he nodded jerkily and rammed the throttle all the way forward. Gifted natural engineer that he was, he hadn't let go of it. The locomotive pounced like a big cat. Hot wind boomed past my ear and the panting of the engine mixed with the chopping sound of the revolving barrels, swallowing it as the reports receded into the distance.

"Bandits!" he shouted.

"Bandits travel light. Would you lug heavy weaponry through the jungle with the authorities on your heels?"

"Who, then?"

I shook my head; but I knew the answer.

The part that concerns me the most is the arms he's supposed to have stockpiled: Gatlings, Napoleons, and a dozen cases of carbines. Judge Blackthorne's words about Oscar Childress, delivered between sips of his quality whisky back in Helena.

We charged full speed for ten more miles before we thought it safe to stop. I'd wound my bandanna around my bleeding hand, and put the throbbing out of my mind as I scouted down the tracks with the rifle to make sure whoever had set up the ambush hadn't stationed more of the same ahead. Back in the coach, Joseph splashed on alcohol from the medical supplies, working so swiftly I was still gasping from the burn when he bound it and tied off the gauze. "There were no doctors in the village where I grew up," he said when I admired the result. "We learned either to tend to ourselves or die from the corruption of the blood."

"Don't forget the pumas."

"I would sooner be eaten by one than by my own rotting flesh."

I couldn't argue with that.

He slid the bottle of alcohol and roll of gauze into the bib of his overalls. "We must sleep in the engine, not here. And one of us must be awake at all times, to mind the gauges and to keep watch." He was silent for a moment. "You are certain about the gun?"

"You saw what it did to the cab."

"Several men with rifles could have done the same."

"On an open firing range. That dense growth would have deflected ordinary rifle rounds. I watched a Gatling demonstration in Fort Benton. Those fifty-caliber slugs took a piece the size of your head out of the stockade wall."

"How could Childress know so soon we were coming?"

"Our friends in Alamos. If what I was told is true, there's no wire service to his plantation. Even if lawyer Bonaparte or Chief Férreo got word to Cabo Falso, no horse and rider could make it back this far in so short an amount a time. One or the other of them must have sent a messenger directly to wherever this band was camped. Is this whole country in cahoots with Childress?"

I tried to open a bottle of Scotch, but I couldn't get a grip with my injured hand. He made a sound of impatience, took the bottle from me, smashed off the neck against the brake handle, and took a swig. Wiping the back of his hand across his lips, he passed it over.

"He is not *El Presidente* Diaz's only enemy. Are you still so interested to hear what this man has to say?"

I drank, swallowed. The spirits crawled up my spine, down my arm, and into the torn heel of my hand, numbing the pain. Up ahead the *Ghost* conserved its strength, its iron heart pumping in measured beats like a lion at rest. "The fire behind, the plague, too, and now a blizzard of bullets. What's a little quiet conversation compared to that?"

He grunted and fisted the bottle. "Here, a man need not burden himself wondering what to do next. The country decides."

We had another bracer apiece, then put the spirits away and got up to leave the coach. It was a relief to get to my feet without dizziness; my strength was back at last, if made a bit more buoyant by alcohol. We filled the canteen from a cask of water, pocketed some tins of food, and requisitioned extra belts of ammunition from the arsenal.

Just before stepping down I turned back and laced my arms through the bails of two buckets of coal oil, and gestured to him to do the same. He did so without question.

We put in another fifteen miles before sundown and pulled onto a siding in a notch that had been blasted into the mountainside to rest. Travel at night was risky, especially with the threat of a tree or a boulder blocking the tracks, either by natural or human design, and Joseph said the line wasn't exclusive to the *Ghost,* for all its loneliness: "The weekly express from Guadalajara is due any month."

Like a garment soaked with sweat in the heat of day, the jungle damp turned clammy after dark. We were warm enough in the blankets we'd brought from the coach, but the cramped quarters of the cab stiffened our muscles and we stirred often, Joseph muttering half-awake oaths in a combination of Spanish and Indian, I more often bumping against something hard and protruding, bruising my scalp, cracking that inconveniently placed knob of bone on the inside of the elbow and sending a wave of pain and nausea all the way up my arm. More than once I thought of stepping down and sleeping on the ground, but I had a horror of cockroaches, so much a part of that country the revolutionists had written them into their anthem. It was no idle fear: When my groin itched I reached down to scratch it, blaming too many days and nights spent in the same clothes, and something the size of a ground squirrel crawled onto the back of my hand. I leapt to my feet, shouting and cracking my skull on the roof of the cab, and shook the thing out into the night.

Joseph opened one eye, the white glistening in ragged moonlight. I told him what had happened.

"You should have waited. He was only looking for a warm place to curl up."

"I'm not in the business of providing shelter for vermin."

"You must learn to accept this country for what it is, and not wish it could be what it is not. Men have gone mad wishing." He turned over and resumed snoring, in that steady, half-pleasant way of the native tribes.

I inspected myself and the blanket for more intruders, gave the blanket a vigorous shake just in case, and lay back down. I didn't know I'd fallen back asleep until I dreamed again of Lefty Dugan. He doffed his hat and bowed his head to show me the hole I'd opened there, shiny as a shotgun bore.

I should of left you to drown in that river, Page.

He wasn't speaking so much as willing the words into my head, where they dropped and lay like dead ash from spent kindling.

My eyes popped open. I'd have slept easier with the roach. I slid out from under the blanket and stepped down, carrying the Whitney rifle. I'd traded the ticking-cap for my hat; the sweatband felt like snail-slime against my forehead. I walked alongside the tracks, paying no attention to things that crunched under my boots. On a cloudless night in the mountains, the stars were as big as Christmas balls, the quarter-moon hanging so close to the earth I could grab its bottom horn with both hands and pull myself up to my chin.

The hours of darkness belonged to the lesser creatures. The din of crickets and tree-frogs was as loud as the Barbary Coast at midnight, with the empty-barrel gulp of the odd bullfrog coming in at intervals so irregular they were impossible to predict; it had waked me every time. In the distance—it might have been my imagination, caused by all our talk—the cry of a hunting cat shredded the heavy overlay of sound like someone tearing canvas.

I don't know how much time I spent walking, but when I stopped and turned back, the train was almost out of sight, its black prow visible only as the silver-blue steam drifted through the slots in the cowcatcher like a phantom passing through solid matter. I trudged back, hoisted myself up by the grab-rail, and wound myself back into the blanket, clutching the rifle as if it would stand off nightmares the way it did men and beasts. The rest of the night was as long as what had come before, and although I slept no more I was glad when first light came. I assumed men who were condemned to hang at dawn welcomed the end of that last night just as much.

NINETEEN

"J*esus Dio!*" **Joseph** hauled back on the brake.

The wheels screamed, showering sparks in fantails on both sides of the cab; one of them landed square on the back of the hand that was still healing. It stung like a wasp, but I hardly noticed it. I was too busy flying backward.

I was an India-rubber ball attached to an elastic band. I slammed against the stacked wood in the tender, the impact slapping my lungs flat. Then the band contracted, pitching me forward; but I was ready for that. I threw my hands against the cast-iron panel with its goggle-eyed gauges, catching myself before my head could go into the open firebox. There I leaned, pumping air back into my chest. I was a broken bellows sucking up shards of glass.

The rest of my senses blinked back on like bubbles popping in thick soup. My vision cleared, the engine wheezed rhythmically, I smelled the sharp odor of steel on steel, identified the sour-iron aftertaste of fear on my tongue. My ears ached from the shrieking of the wheels.

Every curse my father had taught me came to mind, along with some refinements I'd picked up in battle and on the cattle trail, but I choked them back. I respected Joseph's mastery of his machine. Most times he operated it as if the brakes didn't exist. All I could see was his hunched back, seemingly decapitated; he'd stuck his head that far through the opening on the left, straining to peer up the tracks. The muscles on the hand gripping the brake handle were bunched tight, stretching the glove taut.

I peeled my palms away from the front of the cab. The wound was throbbing now, aggravated by the live spark that had burned a hole through the bandage. "Did we hit something?"

No reply. He pried loose his grasp. The handle looked crimped, as if by a pair of powerful pliers. I couldn't remember if it had been that way before, but I wouldn't have been surprised if he'd done it with his fist alone. He blew out a bellyful of pent-up air and hopped down from the cab.

I followed. I thought of the rifle only when I was on the ground. I didn't go back for it. Something about the episode told me it wouldn't be useful.

It wasn't. A great dark heap lay across the tracks, not ten feet from where the locomotive had come to rest. I thought at first part of the mountain had fallen away, and felt the full force of the collision we'd narrowly missed.

Then the wind kicked up, clearing away the steam from the pipes and the smoke from the wheels, and I saw it was no rockslide, although the result wouldn't have been different if we had hit it. Coarse black hair stirred in the current of air, the tips glinting, as if they'd been dipped in silver by a smith.

A slagheap of muscle beneath. I caught another smell then, of rank sweat and suet and something more visceral, thick and pungent, like musty wine gushing from a shattered barrel; the last expulsion of life, spilling out like—

"Guts." Joseph pointed to a glistening red pile a few feet away from the mound, still steaming even in that torpid climate; the last combative gasp of a life lived on its own terms.

I walked around to the front of the thing, which was pointed in the direction of the mountains, the blunt muzzle with its shotgun-bore nostrils raised slightly; inexorably, the brute had been heading for high ground, nose into the wind. The ears were tiny in comparison to the oven-size head, the open eyes like black shoe-buttons; but the corrugated lips were curled back to expose fangs the length and thickness of a man's thumb, defiant even in death. Extinct, the American Grizzly still boiled with savage hate. The remnants of its breath stank of raw fish and fermented juniper berries. I thought of sardines preserved in gin.

Joseph took its left rear paw with its calliope of razor-sharp black claws and lifted it with both hands. The old fellow still had his lungs; they hadn't got them. A gust passed through the reeds of its throat: more rank air, accompanied by a roar, or rather the ghost of one; a sickly thing, almost a bleat, with only the memory of power behind it, but it was enough to shrink my spine. I sprang back; impossible not to, even knowing the source. I'd heard too many stories of hunters slain by a beast they thought was killed.

"He is warm still," the Indian said. "I should say he has not been dead an hour. But he came here with more inside him." His arm swept across the pile of guts; it was too small to account for the size of the cavity. "He was killed and gutted, but to what purpose? The meat remains."

"One of your pumas, interrupted by the train."

"I have never known one to attack a grizzly, let alone win. Also the cat eats from the outside in, starting with the neck and shoulders, then the buttocks. They have not been touched. Always he saves the insides for dessert." He groped the thick mantle of matted fur encircling the massive neck, stopped, probed, then held up a forefinger, stained purple to the second knuckle. "Gunshot wound. Man is the only animal who slays for anything other than food."

"There's only one reason anyone would shoot down a bear on railroad tracks and not take the skin or meat."

Immediately he straightened and joined me in scanning the forest. Birds perched and nested undisturbed among the branches.

"It is not a good place for an ambush," he said. "The undergrowth is too thick, and a man in a tree presents too good a target. One cannot choose where a bear will decide to cross the rails."

"But why take away the guts?"

"*Quien sabe?* The other thing about man is one can seldom judge his actions until it is too late."

The Indian was getting to be tiresome company. He seemed never to grow weary about being right.

Neither of us was foolish enough to attempt to remove eight hundred lifeless pounds from the tracks without a brace of oxen, but after contemplating the immense mound of hair and flesh and gristle and bone I went back to the locomotive and brought two buckets of coal oil. Joseph, catching the significance, did the same, and we spent ten minutes splashing the contents over the carcass, soaking it to the skin; by the time we finished, our eyes were watering from the fumes. He backed up the train another fifty yards for safety's sake while I wrapped a rag around a branch I broke off a tree and saturated it with what was left in the last bucket. I stepped back and touched a match to the rag. It went up with a sucking sound. I cocked my arm and flung the torch at the bear.

Blue flame traced a narrow path through thick hair toward the hump behind the grizzly's neck, and then the rest of the heap caught with a thud that shook the ground. By then I'd retreated almost as far as the train, but I felt the heat all down my front. The flames leapt sixty feet into the air, gushing black smoke that would continue to stain the blank sky long hours after we'd pulled away. My nostrils shrank from the stench of scorched hair, fumes, and roasting meat.

The long coarse guard hairs, designed to shed water, went first, flaring yellow and peeling away from the tan downy undergrowth, like yellowed cotton batting, that kept the animal warm when the mercury fell below zero. Next came the flesh, such a bright pink that many hunters would rather take the hide from a skunk than a bear; the naked carcass looked too much like a freshly skinned human being. I turned away at that point.

We lay over for the night while the obstruction smoldered, taking turns carrying the red safety lantern to flag down any other trains that might approach from behind; it was obvious none would be coming from the other direction, with the fire making a beacon visible for miles.

I fed and watered the bay and walked it along the track away from the burning hulk and its sinister stench. The horse placed its hooves carefully; days aboard a moving train had robbed it of its faith in stationary surfaces. I gave it a sympathetic pat, but just one. That breed of creature and I understood each other too well to expect any greater sign of affection.

The fire was still burning at dawn, but by the time the sun cleared the mountains the bear was a pile of charred bones, stubborn clumps of smoking fur, and simmering puddles of grease. If anything it looked more fearsome in that state, like something prehistoric from a time when the earth was no safe place for man. The hooped rib cage, big as it was—a full-size man could have crawled through it on hands and knees without brushing the sides—brought me back to the abandoned dugout where we'd spent a night, and the bones of the murdered Pinkerton detective, like hollow wooden flutes. He'd made a study of Oscar Childress and wound up a skeleton; the grizzly had attracted his attention or that of someone like him, and ended the same way. I'd been sent to kill him. What was to prevent me from leaving my own bones behind in Mexico?

"Nothing," Joseph said.

I jumped; no matter how civilized an Indian, he always managed to come up on a white man noiselessly. "What?"

"There is nothing here that two men cannot now remove; although I wish I'd thought of sparing the heart before we set fire to it. My people say that to eat the heart of a bear is to inherit some of its strength and courage. Why do you laugh?" he asked then.

I stopped. The sound was strange in my own ears. I hadn't heard it since before I'd crossed the border.

"I wish I'd known that before I ate my first chicken liver."

He snorted and tugged on his gloves. No matter how uncivilized a white man, no Indian will ever share his humor.

We wrapped our bandannas around our faces and cleared away what we could of the debris, breaking often when our gloves started to smolder. At last we took hold of the great leering skull and twisted it this way and that, again and again. The half-incinerated tendons fought us with all the determination of the beast in life, and when finally the skull tore loose with a pop, the sudden release nearly threw us to the ground. We hurled it down the slope. It turned end over end, slow as a ballet, its jaws opening in one last silent roar. When it landed at the base of the foothills, it threw up a geyser of dust and ash. We crossed ourselves in unison.

"What about the ties?" Panting, I stared at the still-glowing timbers supporting the rails.

"The *Ghost* laughs at such things, as we well know."

It didn't; but after a few teeth-clenching moments of wild rocking, the train settled onto the level. Joseph eased the throttle forward and we thundered deeper into the green empty space on the map of the Conquistadors.

III

Cape Hell

TWENTY

We hadn't gone a mile when the sun went out, like a sharp draft blowing out a candle. The sky turned black and the dam broke, simple as that.

We crept through ten miles of rainfall so heavy we might have been rolling along the bottom of the ocean. At noon, the time when under normal circumstances the Mexican sun scoured everything as bright as brass, our headlamp was good for no more than five yards, with the water lancing down through its shaft like silver spikes. The rain was as thick as molasses and nearly as black; Joseph had me light a lantern in order to see the gauges. The air in the cab was so heavy we were breathing each other's exhaust. We took turns leaning out the sides looking for the oncoming lamp of another train or more obstacles on the track, and pulled our heads back in, blinded by water and soaked halfway to the waist; but it was worth it to escape the fug inside.

"The gods have taken a dislike to us," Joseph said, squeezing a puddle onto the floor from his bandanna. "The monsoons are not due for another month."

"The *gods*?" I stressed the plural. Scratch the newly converted and you found a heathen every time.

"Jesus, He is not so *vengativo*; what is the word in English?"

"Vengeful."

"They are weak, the old ones, and so they huddle together in the rain, where the priests cannot ferret them out."

I couldn't argue with his science; but I could inject some of my own. "The same rain is falling on Childress, don't forget."

"We shall see. The seasons are not so *sensato* up here as below."

I saw what he meant an hour later, when we emerged from the deluge as suddenly as if we'd slid through a curtain. Ahead, the sun flashed off the rails and made cracks in the earth on either side of the cinderbed; behind us was a black wall of water. Oven air filled the cab, as stultifying as when we'd been hemmed in by rain.

He leaned forward on the throttle and motioned toward the firebox. I'd just fed it; flames leapt out when I opened the door, heating the space beyond bearing. I looked at him, panting like a parched dog.

"There is a two-mile grade ahead," he said. "Without enough steam we will have to back down to the level and start again."

I poked as many chunks into the box as would fit, the flames licking at my gloves and drawing steam from where I'd stained the left with blood. We swung around a bend—going fast enough, I swore, to lift the landward wheels clear of the track—and began the steady climb; the pistons pumped their elbows, planted their feet, and leaned into the grade. A third of the way up we slowed, slowed some more; the wheels made a noise new to me, a wet sliding sound like a catfish makes when it misgauges a leap, lands on the deck of a boat, and slides across the boards. Just then we stopped moving at all, although I could still hear the wheels turning; in place, with a shrill complaining whine and the drive rods churning—grunting, like an old man grappling with a steep flight of stairs. The cords stood out in Joseph's neck; he had the throttle all the way forward and was still pushing. He wouldn't have shown more strain if he'd loaded the train onto his back and started carrying it himself.

"Grease on the rails," he said through clamped teeth.

I smelled it then, through the wood-smoke and hot oil and steam rolling off scorched metal: a rank stench, as if something had crawled up into the cab and died days before.

The Indian smelled it too. He had both fists on the throttle then, but freed one to touch the four points of his throat, shoulders, and abdomen.

I knew then what he knew: why the grizzly was dead, and what had happened to the rest of its entrails.

They hadn't gotten there on their own. Whoever had gutted the beast had carried them all that way and spread them on the rails where the grade began, to stop the *Ghost* literally in its tracks. My stomach did a slow turn. I forced back bitter bile; and I was ten feet from the source of the reek. I saw in a flash the wretches charged with the task, faces bound and breathing through their mouths.

There came an evil outhouse fetor of boiling offal as the slime reacted to the heat of friction. The wheels spun, but we were stock still.

The trees along this stretch were of much more recent growth than what we'd passed; sometime within the past couple of decades, a fire had cleared several acres, leaving only black earth behind; striplings had sprouted, growing into adolescent trunks spaced far enough apart for a man to squeeze between them on horseback. From the greased grade to the open terrain, the area might have been designed by the patron saint of bushwhackers.

I thrust out a hand and closed it on the engineer's where it gripped the throttle. "Put it in reverse."

He acted without question, hauling the handle back toward his body. The wheels screamed with the sound of metal shearing, the *Ghost* shuddered, violently enough to make me lunge for a handhold; it seemed as if the boiler was about to blow. Then the shaking stopped, steam sighed, and the trees began moving forward. We were backing down the tracks, still slipping a little but moving, if far too slow for comfort.

Then the pounding started again, slugs the size of lumps of coal punching holes in the cab's wooden frame, spanging off steel and iron and kicking up sparks. The bear's carcass had delayed us long enough for the men who'd dropped it there to ride to the spot, measure the range, and set up a nest. This was no catch-as-catch-can operation like the last attack; I ducked just as a shrieking ball of lead passed through the space where my head had been. Thank God I'm not tall.

We were picking up speed. Trains don't go as fast backwards as forward, but gravity was helping out. Joseph left the brake alone. We were doing thirty at least when we hit the level, and when we made it back around the bend he let the throttle out all the way. By then we'd picked up fire from another angle, not as regular as from the Gatling, but from more than a few rifles placed in strategic position. I could picture the snipers arranged in two rows, kneeling in front, standing in the rear, firing in volleys. We crouched below the opening in the cab, I clutching the Whitney across my thighs. It was no good as long as I couldn't risk showing myself long enough to locate a target and take aim from a moving platform, but the solid stock felt good in my hands.

I heard something then, louder than the chugging of the engine: a long shrill splitting noise and a rush of leaves and branches, like a tree lashed by howling wind.

A tree.

Without consulting the engineer I reached up and hauled on the brake handle. Again came the high-pitched cry of locked wheels against the rails, and the sickening lurch of the engine fighting inertia; I'd set my feet so I couldn't be thrown off them in my crouching position, but Joseph had had no warning, and fell back against me; I wobbled, but kept my footing. He fell hard on his buttocks, but his grasp of the throttle prevented him from sprawling all the way onto his back.

A train doesn't stop on the instant, especially with slickum on the wheels. We struck hard enough to shatter branches and send them spinning end over end past the cab, carrying with them the sharp sweet scent of green wood. Another party had stationed itself behind us, and had to have had their axes swinging while we were still slipping on the grade.

I didn't wait for what was coming next. I stuck the muzzle of the rifle through the cab opening on the side of the mountains and squeezed the trigger. Once again I had no hope of hitting anyone or anything; I was gambling for time.

A gamble I lost. When I turned my head to see how Joseph was getting along, the Indian's hand came out of a recess inside the tender on his side of the cab. An ugly pistol pointed at me. The muzzle was as big around as a drainpipe.

I let the rifle fall butt-first to the floor—I'd never clear the barrel through the opening in time—and scooped out the

Deane-Adams; but I knew that was just as futile. Long before I could level it, a sheet of white flame blinded me and I fell as hard as the tree and a lot faster.

***I keep a** pistol in the cab. Not even Joseph knows about it.*

Hector Cansado, the dead engineer, hadn't invented the hidden weapon, but he'd misjudged his fireman. He'd thought to keep it secret by concealing it on the side of the tender opposite the Indian's post, but either Joseph had discovered it earlier or stumbled across it after he took Cansado's place at the throttle.

The glimpse I'd had of it before I blacked out had suggested early manufacture, nearly ancient; percussion arms were a scarce commodity in a nation racked with revolution every few years and in the control of nervous governors with seasoned troops and no laws against search and seizure. This one reflected none of the grace of its era. Built simply of thick steel and all of one piece, the frame curved to fit a man's hand, it was equally effective as a firearm or a bludgeon. As I lay in a watery half-world lanced with splinters of white-hot pain, I didn't know whether I'd been shot or struck over the head.

When I came far enough around to choke back a sudden sharp flash of bitter vomit, I felt the earth moving beneath me. This was nothing new since Montana Territory, but the rhythm was different, less regular; when whatever I was traveling in lurched, sending a burning bolt of agony straight to the top of my skull, I recognized the feel of a wooden wheel plunging into a rut in hard soil. I smelled green wood then, fresh-sawn, heard the hollow plop of shod hooves, and knew I was in a wagon.

And I knew without opening my eyes that I was being watched.

I raised my lids a crack, fighting the urge to flutter them; God alone knew what awaited me when whoever had me realized I was awake. What I saw through a haze of pain and green-tinged sunlight made me think I was still out and dreaming. The face staring into mine was only remotely human. In the shadow of a broad raddled straw brim with green dappling it through the holes, it looked as if someone had gripped it between the jaws of an enormous pair of pliers and squeezed.

I lowered my lids. The eyes in that pinched face, as black and dull as crabapple seeds and nearly as small, seemed to be studying me closely for any sign of awareness. But my sense of smell was more acute than usual. The owner of the face gave off an odor of cedar smoke and something less pleasant: It made me think of the moldy rags swaddling the bones of the Pinkerton in the dank dugout where he'd died. It seemed to have less to do with the clothes the creature wore—shapeless coverings only—than with an inner corruption. It was too strong to have come from just one source. The thing—I supposed it was human—had companions as redolent.

We were moving up, I could tell. My lungs strained to filter oxygen from the thinning air and my head throbbed, partly from the blow, but as much from the pressure of breathing at that altitude. My tongue was wrapped in a cotton stocking. Involuntarily I licked my lips. They were as cracked as dried clay.

A hand made of sinew wrapped around bone slid behind my head and raised it. I gasped in surprise, and before I could close my mouth something splashed into it, tasting of moss and iron and limestone. I nearly choked, but I swallowed. It tasted better than Judge Blackthorne's aged Scotch whisky.

The hand withdrew and my head hit the wagonbed. Light

burst again, nausea flashed, and I blacked out a second time. When I felt again the rocking motion of the bed, I suspected I hadn't been out long, but there was no telling how far we were traveling from sea level. A great weight seemed to be pressing against my chest. The air was getting rarer. Only two types of creature lived so high above the earth: One was Joseph's pumas.

The posters offering reward for joining with Childress had gotten to the Indian finally. He'd come to the realization that as the man who knew how to operate the train he was more valuable than his passenger; but why I was still alive and worth the effort of transporting over that steep terrain eluded me.

When at length I grew weary of pretending to be insensate, I opened my eyes and propped myself up on my elbows. My companion in the wagon was no longer staring at me; he was crumpled in the corner opposite me, one arm dangling over the tailgate and his ragged straw hat tipped over his face. I was grateful for that. Something about those squeezed-together features made me think of a photograph of a shrunken head I'd seen in one of the Judge's travel books. The man wore a bandoleer with heavy-caliber brass cartridges in the loops, but no weapon that I could see, possibly because he was guarding a prisoner who might be tempted to try to disarm him.

A few yards behind the wagon, a pair of mules with gray muzzles towed another vehicle, a two-wheeled oxcart piloted by my keeper's twin brother: At least I hoped there wasn't an entire race of such nightmare creatures living in those mountains. (That hope would be dashed quickly enough.) This one had on a pair of bandoleers crossed on his chest and a machete like the one I'd taken off the guard in Alamos in an open sheath on his belt, the abbreviated blade hanging off the edge of his narrow seat and banging against the side of the footboard.

In the bed behind him sat a man with his back to me, wearing a decrepit straw hat like the others and more ammunition. Past his shoulder, Joseph faced forward with a stout pinon limb across his shoulders, his wrists bound to it with thick hemp and his arms stretched out on both sides, a seated Christ figure with his face twisted into an expression of indescribable agony.

TWENTY-ONE

My **head hurt** worse trying to work it out.

It was like one of those cruel games adults play with children: Is the penny in the right fist or the left? It was in the left last time, but that doesn't mean this time it will be in the right. It might be in the same fist ten times in a row; but wasn't that too much to expect? So you bit your lip and pointed, and you were wrong most of the time because you haven't learned to think outside of a straight line. That came with growing up.

And then there was that rare diabolical adult who pocketed the penny, presenting you with two empty fists.

I'd gone out too abruptly to see where the blow had come from; if it was a blow. I located the pulpy spot on my scalp, but just touching it sent a thrill of pain out in all directions, so I couldn't probe it thoroughly enough to decide if it was a bullet crease or if I'd been struck by a buttstock. Joseph had aimed the pistol in my direction, but whether he pulled the trigger or used it as a bludgeon, or was aiming at something through the opening in the cab—a man trying to board, who managed to shoot or crack me over the head before the Indian fired, if he'd managed to fire at all—was lost.

There were two possible explanations: Either he'd acted in my defense and been taken, or he'd betrayed me and then been betrayed by those he was in league with. Had they, too, decided that a man who would turn against another—Hector Cansado, myself—wasn't worthy of their trust? But in either case, why not kill him outright?

Childress.

I'd said it myself: If the *Ghost* was what he was after, it was useless without a man who knew how to run it. They would have their orders to bring back the engineer alive at whatever cost.

Which left the problem of why they hadn't killed me or left me for dead at the train.

Sitting up enough to look around, I found the craziest theory to be the most plausible. The man guarding me, the man driving the wagon carrying Joseph, and—when he stirred to stretch himself and turned his head my way to work the kinks out of his neck—the man guarding him might have been identical triplets, born to a family of marked ugliness and, if their vapid eyes and slack mouths were any indication of what lay behind, brute stupidity. The same was true of others riding mules and gaunt horses behind and alongside the wagons: two-legged beasts with pinched-in skulls, displaying no more intelligence than the cartridges in their belts. The obvious conclusion chilled me there in the thick, sopping atmosphere of the Sierras. They were all related, or nearly so, bred for generations in the same small community, doubling and redoubling family strengths—force and ruthlessness—and faults—lack of reasoning—until what was left was a race of vicious idiots.

Oscar Childress, it seemed, had given instructions to spare my life as he had with Joseph. Probably he wanted to know what I'd learned and reported home; or—crazy even to consider it—maybe he was as starved for intelligent conversation as I was.

Why wasn't I trussed as well? On the evidence of appearances, our escorts were incapable of deciding I was in too much misery to attempt escape, which I was: Just the thought of crawling over the side of the wagon and taking off on foot through that wild country made the scenery spin around me. More likely it was a tribal thing, and I was immune. There must be Indian blood in anyone living that long so far from villages, but there had been hatred and rivalry between peoples in the New World for hundreds of years before Columbus. With so many guards and in that landscape, the chances of freedom were next to nothing, but it would be only natural to make the journey as painful as possible for a traditional enemy like Joseph.

I didn't ask my throbbing head to explore the situation further just then.

Tethered to the back of the wagon carrying Joseph was my bay. I heard a gurgling, caught a sharp whiff of ferment, and turned to see my driver lowering one of the Judge's bottles, drawing a sleeve across his lips. He hadn't bothered to uncork it, had just knocked off the neck, and a smear of blood on his sleeve told me he hadn't the sense to predict what a jagged shard of glass could do to his mouth. Maybe his brain was too weak to record pain.

Looking around once again, I saw others guzzling from bottles broken the same way, and knew they'd have looted the train of everything they could use: the firearms along with my hip guns, the tins of food, certainly the gold I'd drawn from the bank; but I'd gladly have traded the money to separate these half-humans from the combination of weapons and liquor. They rode spavined, grass-fed mounts with faces as stupid as theirs. Some of the men were singing—humming—moaning—an approximation of some bawdyhouse song or songs, their voices ranging from guttural growls to nasal whines, and the mix of tones, melodies, and off-key renditions of tunes imperfectly remembered fell somewhere between madhouse wails and cats fighting in an alley, or worse: cats and rats tearing at one another for meat. The wheels of the wagons cried out for grease. The din was hellish.

The animals weren't in charge of the zoo, however.

I'd been reluctant to crank my head far enough around to see very much up ahead—it was hurting fine on its own without that, and my guard was still sleeping; passed out, most likely. I didn't want to find out what he was like with a skull full of drunk's regret. But when a rider came trotting back to smack a dozing idiot's thigh with a leather crop, I saw a man with regular features and fierce black muttonchops wearing a campaign hat stained black with sweat and a gray tunic with the cuffs buttoned back to expose a yellow lining: the contrasting colors were faded almost to the same shade, the fabric darned and patched all over, but the stovepipe boots gleamed black above dusty insteps. Gold braid, faded also, made loops on his sleeves, and on his collar glittered the insignia of a captain of the Confederacy, the engraving worn nearly smooth, but the brass highly polished. The left side of his face was white and shiny, in sharp relief to his deep sunburn, cutting a bare patch from his whiskers, and the eye that belonged on that side lay on some old battleground, leaving behind an empty socket, the flesh around it shrunken to the bone.

I remembered that the nucleus of Childress' private army

comprised members of his old command. This one, whose burnsides were tipped with gray like the coat of the dead grizzly, drew back his hand with lightning reflexes to avoid being bitten by the man he'd jolted out of sleep, but I heard his teeth snap together inches from the flesh. The captain responded with a backhand swipe, striping the man's face with a red welt. He blinked, but apart from laying his own hand on the machete on his belt showed no other physical reaction. If he'd had a tail (and I wouldn't have bet against it), he'd have tucked it between his legs.

The officer cantered back another hundred yards, casting his one-eyed iron gaze along the procession, then wheeled his mount—a muscular sorrel fattened on grain, unlike the others', with sleek haunches—and galloped the other direction to resume his post in the lead.

The parade wasn't heavily populated, but it was strung out for a quarter-mile. As we climbed, the vehicle bringing up the rear rose into view from below a grade. It rolled on tall, iron-felloed wheels, a bundle of ten blue-steel barrels mounted on a wooden crosspiece. As a weapon of wholesale slaughter the Gatling should have been ugly, but it had been hand-crafted by masters, the weight and balance of its wheels allowing it to roll smoothly, almost gracefully over the rude terrain, its brass fittings flashing in the sun. Some of the deadliest vipers are among the most beautiful things in creation.

Joseph, whose own groans of pain had subsided, swayed and pitched with the motion of his wagon, his eyes closed and his chin on his chest. He'd either passed out or died.

Just then his guard cocked a leg and dealt him a blow that left the clear outline of a bootheel on his temple. He snapped to. Pink-tinged drool dripped off his chin, but the whites of his eyes showed briefly before they closed again.

A toad had climbed into my mouth, bloated and sluggish. It was my tongue. My guard had shifted again in his sleep, exposing the stiletto-sharp neck of a bottle sagging in the side pocket of his threadbare canvas coat. There was no sign of the water vessel he'd let me drink from before. Had I dreamt it? The whole trip, it seemed, had been the product of bad whisky and tainted oysters. But liquid was liquid.

I leaned over until my shoulder touched the wagonbed, stretched my arm across the boards until my fingers just touched the neck. I didn't want to slide closer. Animals have instincts, and what he lacked in brainpower he might make up for in the physical senses. I teased the bottle loose slowly, a fraction of an inch at a time, until I could grasp it firmly and slide it free of the pocket.

As I did so, my shirtcuff snagged something. The guard stirred, whimpered. I caught my breath and held it. He opened his mouth, smacked his lips, and snored so rackingly I felt it in my own torn gullet. I let out a bellyful of air and concentrated my attention on freeing the cuff without dropping the bottle. When I pulled gently, something gave: One of the fifty-caliber Gatling shells had come loose from a loop on his belt. I turned my wrist, still holding the bottle by its neck, and curled my little finger around the flanged receiver. With that grip secure I lifted away bottle and round of ammunition in one movement.

I turned the cartridge around in my fingers. The brass shell alone was four inches long and an inch across the base, with the conical lead bullet adding another two and a half inches to its length. Just holding it made me shudder. One of those slugs had come within a handspan of taking my head off.

I put it in a pocket. I had no idea what I was going to do with it, but its weight was reassuring. It was as heavy as a roll of quarters.

There was only a trickle left in the bottle, and just then I'd have traded a carload of the Judge's aged Scotch for as much water as could be wrung from a sponge; but it was all I had available. I closed my cracked lips gingerly around the broken neck and tipped the contents over my tongue. They burned like acid, but I lapped up every drop, stuck my finger as far inside as I dared, wiped it along the glass, and licked it. I lowered the bottle to the boards and let it roll to a stop against the sleeping guard's hip. I lay back, as exhausted as if I'd been pulling the wagon myself.

I dozed, woke; dozed again, and dreamed I was back in Virginia, desperate for rest but bombarded by mosquitoes the size of gypsy moths, whining like mortar shells and stinging like the dull needles military orderlies used to prevent smallpox, wallowing in a puddle of my own sweat in a tent rank with mildew. We were on our way to a place called Cold Harbor, as poorly named a destination as ever there was. I'd been born in the high chill dry air of the Bitterroots, and would never accustom myself to inhaling oxygen as through a moldy bandanna. I jerked myself awake by sheer will—and started shivering. My teeth chattered so loudly I wanted to clasp my hand over my mouth to avoid drawing the attention of my witless beast of a guard; wanted to, but hadn't the strength to lift my arm from the wagonbed.

That's when I learned what I've known ever since: Once a victim of malaria, always a victim, at intervals no physician could predict, no matter how well-trained.

And higher we climbed. I looked up at the black-winged things wheeling in circles against white sky and felt I could reach out and pluck a feather.

TWENTY-TWO

Time is measured by clocks, calendars, the turning of the earth and the shifting of constellations, none of which was capable of marking our passage up those mountains. I woke abruptly, and lay for a moment wondering what was responsible, until I realized we'd stopped. I'd grown so accustomed to the pitch and sway of the wagon and the shrieking of the ungreased axles that the sudden cessation of noise and motion had come as rudely as a pistol report. Dusk was all about, turning the sky the shade of eggplant, the zigzag treetops flat black, as if they'd been stamped against it with printer's ink. I wondered if we'd stopped to rest the animals. The thought that the ghastly shades who commanded them needed to halt for any human reason was too unlikely to consider.

It was dusk, yes: *A* dusk, anyway. There was no telling how many had come and gone since those two insignificant things, guts from a dead bear and a felled tree, had succeeded where nothing else could, stopping the *Ghost*. Nearer ground level, wriggles of yellow and orange suggested flames, spaced too evenly apart to belong to anything so random as nature. They twisted and snapped atop narrow posts stuck in the ground, illuminating a broad one-story building pale with whitewash, pierced at regular intervals with paned windows, dark shutters folded flat against the walls, and a proper shake roof. Peering over the side of the wagon, I swept the sweat from my eyes with the heels of my hands, but when I looked again it was still there, a cozy domestic arrangement, with bowls of flowers hanging by chains from a long front porch containing a bentwood rocker and a wicker table. All it lacked was a pitcher of lemonade to complete the effect. Between the torches, I identified similar posts supporting pale oblong shapes: gourds, set up possibly for target practice, although they looked too close to the house for safety.

Half of it, of course, was delirium. The building had to be an illusion. Such a house, the grass around it shorn close to the ground, with homey yellow light glowing through the glass and a blue-enamel mounting block resting beside the flagstone walk, had been transported there in my fever from a neighborhood in St. Louis or Denver, within walking distance of a schoolhouse and a church. It no more belonged in that wild place than a hopscotch court on Cemetery Ridge. The gourds were homely enough to be real.

I was wrong about both, as it turned out; but by then I knew I'd been wrong about almost everything connected with Oscar Childress from the start.

As the creatures dismounted and milled about, unhitching harnesses and opening their trousers to spill acrid-smelling water onto the ground—I swore steam rose from it, although the evening was warm—I looked for Joseph, but by then it had grown too dark to see inside the wagon that had been carrying him. Once again my gaze went toward that impossible house. Piled up against a side wall, just visible in the shifting light of the torches, was a pale heap that struck a gong deep in my memory.

In my ranch hand days I'd supported myself winters hunting buffalo, then switched to wolfing and traded the pelts for bounty. The packs had swollen on the easy pickings of the shaggies' abandoned carcasses, and when they'd stripped them to the bone, armies of vagabonds had swarmed in to harvest the skeletons for sale to manufactories back East, which fashioned them into buttons, combs, and handles for knives and chests of drawers and pulverized them to press into china for the table and to filter the impurities from sugar. Within months of the last hunt, the plains were scraped clean of any evidence the beast had ever existed, millions vanished in twenty short years. I'd led pack horses piled with wolf pelts through city streets turned into canyons of bone; but soon even they vanished. Where Childress had managed to find so many to refine his coarse-ground cane was another of the mysteries that piled up around him like—well, the bones themselves.

I heard the *shink* of a pin being drawn from an iron staple, followed by another, and then the tailgate swung down with a rattle and thump of elmwood. A toe struck me in the ribs, shooting a red flare of pain all the way to my torn scalp. My keeper, awake at last, stood stretching, his own bones making as much noise as the tailgate. I pulled myself to my feet before he could aim another kick. I was wearing my old comfortable range Stetson, trained to my head so it wouldn't blow off in a stiff wind, but I held the brim as I made to step down, because the angle I'd chosen to avoid contact with the sticky lump wasn't natural. I steadied myself with the other hand on the side of the wagon as I groped for the ground with one foot. Standing on bare earth I couldn't feel my legs. I took a couple of steps to get the blood flowing, but instead of the pins and needles I expected my knees folded and I pitched straight forward into black.

At first I thought the whole business of the house and the torches and the pile of bones and the stop itself was a dream, and actually felt the familiar lurching of the wagon; but there was something different, almost alien, about the surface where I lay on my back. I hadn't slept in the upholstered berth aboard the train in days, and had no idea how long I'd spent stretched out on the weathered boards of the wagon. My muscles and bones had adapted themselves to unyielding planks, beginning with the floor of the locomotive's cab, to the point where the softness of feathers, ticking, and clean linen—it smelled of cornstarch and fresh air—made them ache. Whoever had carried me here would have been kinder to have laid me on a floor, then a stiff bench, and brought me by degrees to occupy a civilized bed.

Just where the bed was I couldn't say, even when I opened my eyes. Darkness surrounded me, so black it made my heart clatter. I was sealed inside a padded coffin; cedar, from the sweet scent. I lay breathing shallowly, to avoid exhausting what air was left me, dreading to raise a hand and confirm the tightness of my confinement. My hand twitched, lifted an inch, dropped back to my chest. I pressed my lips tight and willed it to rise again. My arm went up and up and felt nothing but empty air. I opened my mouth wide, exhaled in a whoosh, and sucked in, filling my chest until it ached. I felt as if I'd dived into a thousand-foot lake, touched the bottom, and clawed my way back to the surface with my lungs straining through the last fathom close to bursting. The air was even sweeter than it smelled.

Gradually—glacially—my eyes adjusted themselves, allowing a gray glimmer of light to measure the dimensions of the room where I lay and to suggest a shape for the objects that shared it with me. It was either windowless or the curtains were heavy, because the only source of illumination was a hollow rectangle at the far end where a door didn't fit flush to the frame. I had no idea if it was day or night, or if the space beyond was lit by the sun or a lamp. It reflected on the curvature of a pitcher near my head, and fell from there to the top of a table or a nightstand within reach of where I lay. Through the corner of my eye I made out a bedpost, curved also, but not well enough to decide whether it was wood or metal, only that it, too, was capable of reflecting light.

They fascinated me, those polished surfaces. Apart from the glass-bezeled gauges and steel of the *Ghost* and the rails it rolled on, it had been days since I'd laid eyes on anything that wasn't coarse and light-absorbing; even the lush fittings of the parlor car were a dim memory since I'd decamped to the front of the train.

Something else glittered, as if from its own source of light; the gilded binding of a leather-bound volume lying beside the pitcher on its stand. I brought my face close to the spine and peered, but the room might have been black as pitch for all I could make of the gold-stamped title: It was German. That gave me a good idea of whose bed it was. Two people in that vicinity might understand English and Spanish; it was unlikely more than one would be educated in any other language.

I decided it was night. The air was chill at that altitude

without the sun to warm it, and wrapped my face in a cold mask. My arm, cold too, was bare where it lay on a coverlet made from the pelt of some animal and cured to silken softness; doeskin, I thought. Between it and my body was a linen sheet, woven so finely it felt like heavy cream. It covered my other arm. I slid my hand down my body, confirming my suspicion that I was naked.

I felt weak, but my skin was cool and dry. There was no determining how long I'd been there, or how many times I'd been bathed of sweat and the bedding had been changed. Malaria has been with me off and on in all the years since, and the time needed for the fever to break varies. It might have been hours or days.

Carefully, to avoid triggering a relapse, I peeled aside the coverlet and sheet, sat up, gathered energy, and swung my feet to the floor. That amount of effort took as much out of me as I had for the moment; I leaned my shoulder against the bedpost to collect my strength. My bare soles rested on thick wool, a woven rug probably of Indian workmanship. I worked my toes, enjoying its warmth. I'd begun to shiver, and to worry that another attack was on its way.

When the sensation faded, I found the courage to test the extent of my recovery. I shifted my weight forward, grasped the bedpost, and pulled myself upright. The room did a slow turn but ended up stable. I tugged the sheet off the bed, wrapped it around me, closing it at my throat, and went exploring.

Some kind of decoration hung on a wall, a large painting, I thought, but the subject, painted in dark colors and possibly made more murky with age, remained anonymous inside a frame of some dark lustrous wood.

Beyond the edge of the rug the floor was wooden as well, cool and smooth under my unshod feet. There was pine aplenty in the Sierras, and evidently labor sufficient to cut and split and plane and sand it. Such mindless and repetitive work would be ideal for the tiny brains of the men who'd brought me there.

I bumped into something tall and solid. I laid a palm against the door of a wooden cabinet. The cedar smell increased when I pulled it open. I groped inside, felt fabric. I hadn't been out of my canvas coat in a week, and knew the texture even in the dark. Probing further, my hand found the Gatling cartridge in the pocket where I'd put it. My relief was tinged with revulsion: Who'd be senseless enough to overlook it when he was undressing me, if not one of my doltish escorts? The thought of his hands touching my bare skin made it crawl. It was as if a snake had slithered over me while I slept.

The rest of my clothes, gritty as they felt from constant wearing, were as welcome as the coat with its secret treasure. I let the sheet fall to the floor and stood naked in the stiff Mexican night. I dressed slowly, pacing myself, sitting on the bed to pull on my boots. The effort spent me. I lay back for a few minutes to refuel. I wasn't quite as weak as a kitten, but I fell short of a full-grown tabby.

Whoever had hung up my things hadn't been accommodating enough to leave behind my revolvers; but there was no need to be greedy. The fifty-caliber slug slapped pleasantly against my hip when I put on the coat.

I had a fair notion where I was: the plantation headquarters of Major Oscar Childress, thousands of feet almost straight up from Cape Hell.

TWENTY-THREE

My hat occupied a top shelf of the cabinet, still damp with sweat. That was encouraging; I hadn't been out of my senses more than a day or two or it would be dry. I'd been in that state before, once when a bullet grazed my scalp and a few times when the horse under me decided I didn't belong and pitched me headfirst into the American frontier. It was always like reading a book with pages torn out, and a relief to know it wasn't missing anything beyond a couple of chapters.

The thought of old head injuries reminded me to check my scalp. My temples were throbbing, but that could have been part of the fever. I fingered the tender spot carefully, felt woven cloth, and around it bare skin. Someone had shaved a tonsure some two and a half inches square and patched it with gauze.

I couldn't picture any of Childress' half-animals performing that operation, or bothering to consider it. The image of poor Joseph, traitor or not, crucified in the back of a wagon was as vivid as when I'd first seen it. If the major had added physician to his long list of skilled occupations, he was a da Vinci for the nineteenth century.

I slid a hand inside my pocket and closed it around the Gatling round, purely for security. I still didn't know what to do with it, but it was the only secret I had left.

Approaching the rectangle of light I hesitated, then groped for a handle. It was a knob, engraved bronze or brass from the feel. It would be locked, naturally. Naturally I paused again when it turned without resistance and a latch slid free with the slight friction of metal scraping metal.

Caution be damned. I'd been carried up the mountain for a purpose, and if it was important I stay in that room the door wouldn't have been left open. I swung it wide and entered a library.

It was rigged out like the shelves in a ship, with wooden lips attached to keep the books from falling. Were earthquakes common at that altitude? The shelves were pine; tiny cones of sawdust had been left by termites, but the books themselves were in good condition, although they showed traces of use. The titles were printed on cloth and stiff paper and stamped in gold leaf into leather old and shabby and oiled and glistening: *The Origin of Species by Means of Natural Selection*, *Selected Poems of Robert Browning*, odd numbers of the Encyclopedia Britannica, *Frankenstein*, a shelf of Dickens, *The Anatomy of Melancholy*, bound copies of *The Lancet*, *Principles of Steam*, *Alice in Wonderland*, Clausewitz, *The Oregon Trail*. I didn't linger over the ones in German, French, Latin, and some hen-scratches that were either Hebrew or Greek, but I'd heard of Nietzche somewhere and knew Julius Caesar had had something to say about how Gaul was divided. There were many more, hundreds more, on adjoining shelves all around the room, but they were lost in gloom. It was a hodge-podge of science, history, fiction, philosophy, and poetry, arranged in no order I could apply, either by author or subject, as if they'd been flung randomly into place after consulting, like oranges squeezed dry.

It wasn't just show. I'd visited the libraries of wealthy self-made men and seen their immaculate sets, the spines uncreased and bought by the yard to impress visitors not observant enough to note the fact they'd arrived unopened from the dealers and stayed that way. Waiting—which is what you spend most of your time doing where important people are involved—I'd taken down dozens of them to kill time, only to find most of the pages uncut. Plainly these books had been opened and shut scores of times, their spines thumb-blurred and the bindings loose. Someone had underscored whole passages of Shakespeare in iron-gall ink. The reader had marked his place in Act IV, Scene II of *Richard III* with a Confederate two-dollar bill. I snapped shut the hefty volume—all tragedies—and slid it back into its slot, not before a tarantula scampered out and vaulted up to the top shelf.

The hour was later than I thought; or earlier. A gap in the heavy curtains covering one of a pair of tall windows let in the tarnished light of either dawn or dusk. I walked up to it, spread the heavy green panels, and looked at a crescent of brilliant orange stuck to the edge of a shadowy mountain. I guessed we were in the middle of the range, and having no other means of sensing direction couldn't determine whether I was looking east or west. I waited. It seemed to me the sun was moving up rather than down. When a yellow ray sprang free I knew it was the former. Dawn comes late in the mountains. That made the time nearer six o'clock than five. I was alone, but wouldn't be for long. In the Sierra Madre, no one sleeps in.

The window was unbarred, but as the land fell straight down from the foundation for several hundred dizzying feet, no bars were necessary. It was a large room, three times as long as it was deep, like the inside of a train station, and must have taken up the entire back half of the house; if it was the house I'd seen when our caravan stopped. A rug of Indian design covered the pine floor to within a foot of the walls, with a thunderbird spreading its square wings in silver-gray on a background of red and black. The wool looked as soft as the one I'd walked on barefoot in the bedroom. Paintings in massive gilt frames leaned out on wires from the walls between bookshelves: Portraits with brass nameplates of Thomas Jefferson, John Marshall, and Robert E. Lee, Virginians all; the *Monitor* and the *Merrimack* chucking smoke and fire at each other at Hampton Roads.

Across from the battle scene, a replica of the Conquistador map I'd seen in the Judge's chambers hung uncovered by glass in a snakewood frame. No, I thought, when I stood close: It was no replica, but an original, drawn on either parchment or the skin of some unborn animal, signed in copperplate by a Spaniard whose name I couldn't pronounce. Ancient silverfish had munched the corners round.

A ton of what were no doubt native elk antlers swung from the ten-foot ceiling on a heavy chain, tangled inextricably, cold tallow candles skewered on their points. Between the windows stood a cherrywood desk supported by carved gryphons, on it an amethyst-shaded banker's lamp, a green baize blotter, a Bible the size of a Missouri River ferry, cigars in a bell jar, a blobby bronze inkstand, and a tired grapefruit with a bristle of horsehair pens stuck in it like arrows in Custer's corpse. A quilted leather chair with a hickory frame mounted on a swivel stood at attention behind the desk.

The walls not hidden behind books were rush-covered, the material probably harvested from ponds and marshes, laid out to dry, tea-stained, and woven on looms. Everything in the room, except the books and a great glass globe cradled in maple, seemed to have been fashioned from local resources. It seemed familiar, yet remote, like something I'd read in a book. I was illiterate compared to the man who used that room, but when you've spent much of your life snowed in, you're no stranger to reading. I just couldn't remember which book. It hadn't ended well for the hero.

A fire burned—in that climate—behind mica inserts in an enameled parlor stove. If it had been kindled for my benefit, the connecting door should have been open.

I smelled good tobacco. I've never gotten the habit, but I knew the aroma of the cigars Judge Blackthorne had brought in by boat and train from Havana, and the air here smelled even more refined.

"I grow it myself," said a voice behind me. "Just a small patch, for my pipe; I can't spare any more because of the amount of land the cane needs to flourish. The curing is done by one of those revenants you've met. It's ideal work for creatures without wits. Their capacity for undistracted concentration is remarkable."

I turned to look at the man who'd entered through a side door. He was bald, as I'd predicted he'd be, based on his receding hairline in an old tintype; but I'd been wrong about his going native. A man like Oscar Childress, I saw instantly, would expect nature to go his way rather than the other way around.

TWENTY-FOUR

He wore conventional dress, if the conventions of Boston, Denver, and San Francisco were in order: a black morning coat, striped trousers, dove-gray gaiters. He lacked only a cravat, having buttoned his shirt to his throat. As there was some swelling there, the beginnings of a goiter or dropsy, there was no room for it. Beyond that, his skull was obvious beneath a layer of skin no thicker than the sap from a rubber tree, and the skin itself the dead gray of stagnant water. His eyes, glistening plums floating in deep sockets, were brilliant, with the unnatural brightness of a star burning itself out. That explained the stove; it was there for a sick man, after all. Here was a man dying, who would no more conquer Mexico City than a leper groping for alms with a hand without fingers. I smelled the corruption as surely as from the dead grizzly on the rails, but the exact location of the cancer was a mystery, only that it was the cause.

My journey was useless; if killing Childress to prevent a second Civil War had been why I'd undertaken it.

He joined me before the map. At that range the odor was feral.

"It's fashionable to poke fun at those old cartographers who swarmed the uncharted regions with monsters. They didn't believe in them any more than you or I. It was a ruse to frighten others from the treasures they knew were there."

I was about to ask him what he used in place of monsters when something shook the floor at my feet. The books on the shelves jumped against the strips of wood that restrained them, and I knew then their purpose. A deep bellowing explosion came on the heels of the shake, and something the size and shape of a barrel hoop drifted past the window from which I'd drawn the curtains. I hadn't seen the smoke ring from a discharged cannon since Lee's surrender. The silvery thin strains of a bugle followed, distorted by distance and the irregular topography.

Childress was watching me. His pale eyes were bordered by paler lashes. "I order it fired three times a week. I wanted to conserve powder, but having the brutes practice less often was a mistake. Captain McCready had to re-teach them the rudiments every time. During reveille is best. It's important to keep the experienced troops on edge, and necessary to pound the lesson into the empty heads of the others."

"McCready's the officer with one eye?"

"He lost it at Petersburg. It's disconcerting, I know. I ordered him to wear a patch, but he said the itching was a distraction. I'd rather not risk it in the heat of battle."

He approached the desk, his back straight as from disciplined effort, and stroked the mirror finish. "I don't expect you to appreciate this item. It belonged to a marshal of France.

He brought it with him to New Orleans when he fled the Bourbons. I bought it by telegraphic bid at his estate auction and had it shipped by rail to Cabo Falso and hauled up here by wagon. There was a revolution on at the time, and some men lost their lives in the endeavor. I like to think it a vessel for their wandering souls."

"I'm sure they'd appreciate it." So he was insane as well as physically ill. I'd considered the possibility; but it's one thing to assume and another to experience it at first-hand.

Someone tapped gently and a woman entered, a Yaqui I thought, wearing a muslin blouse and a flowered skirt, huaraches on her bare feet. She carried a silver decanter and china on a tray, which she set on the desk. Her face and hands were as gnarled as an old root.

"Coffee?" Childress offered. "I'm forced to barter for it in Central America. I tried growing my own, but it won't cooperate at this altitude. I couldn't afford the acreage in any case. Sugar's greedy."

I realized then I wasn't thirsty anymore; someone had seen to that while I was suffering. But just the rich smell seemed to level off the pounding in my head. I accepted a cup and sat balancing it on its saucer in a straight chair facing the desk. The china was paper-thin; my fingers made shadows on the other side of the rim. He dismissed the woman, seated himself in the leather chair, rummaged inside the top drawer, and poured white powder from a paper into his cup, stirring it with a tiny spoon. He patted his flat belly.

"A bromide. After all these years I can't get used to the local diet." He sipped the steaming brew. His eyes brightened further. He'd lied; I wondered if he grew his own coca leaves, and if the sugar cane resented them. "You're here to kill me," he said.

If he'd expected to ambush me with that one, I disappointed him. For all I knew his chain of spies extended as far as Helena. I fell back on the original lie.

"I'm not a hired gun. Washington's heard some things, and I was sent to hear them myself, from the horse's mouth if possible, and report back."

"And yet I was told you came to offer me a train in return for a commission with my irregulars."

It came as no shock that Blackthorne had furnished me with two lies of my own, the second to cover the first. An experienced tactician would expect a ruse, and possibly be satisfied once he'd exploded it. It was another example of which fist held the penny.

I sipped from the cup. The coffee was strong but not bitter; he'd made a good trade. "If you found out as much about me as I did about you, you saw through that one right away. What if you succeed in commandeering the Mexican Army and reversing Appomattox? After you conquer a country you have to govern it. What would I be then, attorney general? I've never been comfortable on that side of a desk."

"You can report that everything Washington heard is true. I intend to capture Mexico City, annex the federales, and invade El Paso. Once you control the border, you control international trade. The *Ghost* stays here. It will expedite securing supplies and provisions, and once I've acquired the additional rolling stock, I can have my troops in the capital in half the time—when they're ready."

"Those animals who brought me here never will be."

"I'll lend you my Machiavelli. Cannon fodder wins wars. Once the enemy has spent itself on that carrion, my professionals will be rested and ready to take the field."

"Is this to be a four-year education or a crash course? In other words, how long are you holding me?"

"You've been very ill, and the rainy season is almost upon us. If you set out tomorrow, you'd never make it to Cabo Falso alive."

"What about Joseph? My engineer," I said, when he showed no reaction.

He drew a plain steel watch from his waistcoat, popped the lid, and put it back. The bones of his hands showed through the skin on the backs as clearly as my own fingers through his china; the bright eyes bulged slightly as he pushed himself to his feet. Apart from that he dissembled the expenditure of energy required. "Come with me."

I got up and followed him out the door he'd come in through. A narrow hallway, properly plastered and painted green, led the way to the front of the house between more portraits of prominent Virginians suspended from a picture rail ending in another door. It opened onto one end of the front porch. There hung the flowering plants of my fever-dream; there was the rocking chair and table, and just visible at the opposite end of the porch the curve of the great heap of bones. The torches placed in front, extinguished now, looked like oversize burnt matches, smelling of coal-oil rather than sulphur, and between them the objects I'd thought had been set on their posts to perform as rifle targets. In the light of day they were human skulls.

It was no wonder I'd taken them for gourds. The temples were sunken, as if the meat had been scooped out, and they sloped back shallowly from just above the beetled brows. They were human, but just barely. I'd made the trip up the mountain in the company of their brothers.

Childress saw me looking at them. "I gave up trying to discipline them by rewarding good behavior. The brutes respond only to fear, and while the concept of death itself is beyond their understanding, they share with the rest of us a terror of the unknown."

As he spoke, a pair of his creatures came around the end where the bones were piled with a third between them, his wrists behind his back. Dressed as they all were, in identical shapeless white shirts and trousers, tall boots, bandoleers, and tattered straw sombreros, heads concave on both sides, expressions vapid, I was more convinced than ever that they were related in an unhealthy way.

"What are they?" I asked.

"Revenants. Animated corpses. I rescued them from starvation in an extinct village carved into the side of a mountain by ancient ancestors they don't know ever existed. The women are housed in a building attached to the sugar refinery. They're useless in most of what's required of the sex except the obvious, so I keep them to placate the men. If it weren't for grass and small game slow enough to slay with rocks, they wouldn't have lasted long enough for me to recruit them. They do the sort of work that frees up their betters for more worthy duty.

"I can't tell you what tribe they belong to. I doubt they could themselves, as they're barely capable of speech in any language; everything human has been bred out of them through generations of incest. But they retain all the resentments inherent between the tribes, which is why your man was so mistreated against my orders. That's another reason I keep them around, as subjects of study. Why reasoning should perish and fear and hatred remain as potent as ever is a question no one has answered."

The man with his hands behind his back was forced to kneel

in front of the blue enamel mounting block alongside the flagged path. His wrists, I saw then, were bound with a thong. Without protest, he laid his cheek on the block.

"I don't even know if he's the one responsible for that crude punishment," Childress said. "The brutes all look alike, and I suspect they can't tell even one another apart. I gave up having them whipped for their misbehavior; their minds are so weak they are either unable to feel pain or to connect it with their actions. In any case the lesson is lost. So I teach by example."

He thrust two fingers into the corners of his mouth and blew an ear-splitting whistle. Slow as erosion the two men standing turned their heads in the direction of the noise. He jerked a palm up from his waist. Another long pause before one of them separated himself from the others, slouched back around the bonepile, and returned a moment later supporting Joseph's weight on his shoulders. The engineer was hollow-cheeked, his head down and his hair in his eyes. The soles of his boots scraped the earth. He was barely able to lift them.

By then the major's whistle had summoned a crowd. From either end of the house and from below the drop of the mountain, Childress' creatures shambled into a rough formation strung out facing the house. Hoofbeats pounded, and then some stragglers joined it, driven over the incline by Captain McCready aboard his well-fed sorrel, herding them with his head cocked to one side to monitor them with his single eye. The man who'd brought Joseph mounted the steps to the porch, half-carrying his charge. At another signal, he turned him to face the group. Very slowly, Joseph raised his chin. He may have seen me out the corner of his eye, but he showed no recognition.

"They react to sight and sound," Childress said. "Those

senses are remarkably acute. Unfortunately, their memories are poor clay. I have to keep repeating examples to refresh their understanding."

I made no answer. He was treating me as some kind of student, perhaps an apprentice.

McCready swung down from the saddle and snapped a hand to the brim of his campaign hat. "Sir."

"Proceed, Captain."

He drew a saber from the scabbard on his belt. The sun, clear now of obstructions, flashed off the gold chasing on the blade. He raised it. The man standing over the man with his head on the mounting block drew his short-bladed machete and lifted it as if in imitation. It may have been just that, an ape's duplication of a gesture by a member of a superior race.

I'd seen hangings, fought hand to hand, slain men, without flinching. When the captain's sword swung down, I turned my head away before the machete followed; but I heard the thump and roll, and a collective gust of air from dozens of primitive throats in response. It sounded exactly like the feeble roar the slain grizzly had made when its remains were disturbed.

I despised myself for looking away. I had no authority in that country, but as Blackthorne had told me often enough I was an agent of justice. If I could stand by while a helpless man was beheaded without trial, I could damn well witness the act.

The body lay without twitching, slumped sideways to the ground, the earth stained around the stump of its neck; there's no violent eruption after the initial severance, despite what they write in sensational fiction. The head, looking hardly less aware than it had in life, lay a few yards away where it had come to rest.

I hadn't seen the worst yet.

Captain McCready pointed his saber at two of the men assembled, who came forward to hoist the corpse by its wrists and ankles and bear it around the far corner of the house. Their vacant faces offered no indication that they connected the burden with anything more than a pile of sod.

The captain mounted, cantered over to the head, leaned down, and skewered it deftly with his saber. The sorrel was a trained warhorse: Apart from distending its nostrils during the grisly operation, it showed no reaction. It wheeled at the kick of a heel and trotted up to the line of skulls on display, where the rider plucked one free and, resting it against his pommel, removed the dripping head from the blade and jammed it onto the sharpened pike. He leaned over again to plunge the point of the weapon into the earth, cleansing it, and returned it to its scabbard.

He rode the length of the porch, the horse stepping high, neck curved in a Grecian arch. There was something obscene even in that, an arrogant coddled mount prancing as in an Independence Day parade. The skull it carried had every reason to leer.

McCready scooped up the skull, tossed it onto the mountain of bones, and swung round to salute the major.

"Muster 'em out, Captain."

The dullards dispersed, feet dragging—another second lost between their brains and their extremities and they'd have toppled forward from the waist—but I paid them small attention.

It wasn't so much the spectacle of that nightmare rider,

whose own hollow eye-socket resembled so closely those of the martially aligned skulls, or even the casual disposal of human remains, like slops emptied into an alley. I'd seen as bad in the most vicious war ever fought between man and man. This was more barbaric still. Plainly the dead man's body had been borne no farther than that same pile. And I knew now the source of the bones Childress ground to refine his sugar, and probably shape into the fine china cup I'd sipped from minutes ago.

My stomach did a slow roll, my vision blurred; black petals blossomed in the haze. But I remained upright, either by sheer force of will or because inch by inch I was becoming accustomed to darkness.

TWENTY-FIVE

Joseph's escort turned him toward the front door. The beast-man's strength was ten times his ability to think; he bore 160 inert pounds, inches from the ground, as easily as a sack of grain. I asked Childress where Joseph was being taken.

"To an ambulance, and from there to a fully equipped infirmary. I'd have had you brought there, but you were in worse condition, if you can believe it, and might not have survived the journey. These Indians are hardy. He needs hydration and nourishment administered under close supervision and a dose of cinchona, just in case. The natives have used it to treat malaria for two hundred years, but it's been slow to catch on outside Mexico. I sent a paper to *The American Medical Journal*, but it was ignored, probably because of my affiliations. Medical science should rise above petty politics. As a beneficiary, perhaps you can make the case for the remedy."

"I'll do my best; assuming I don't die of the cure."

"It's not a cure. You'll revisit the symptoms again and again throughout your life, but they'll not be fatal. You came through the first time, thanks to the bark, and the chances are you'll survive the others. Once your friend has recovered, he'll share quarters with you in the barracks. I'm looking forward to having my own room back. Captain McCready is a fine officer, but he snores like a steam shovel. Are you up to a tour of the grounds?"

"Have I a choice?"

I'd transgressed. He looked at me with the expression of a host whose guest had insulted his accommodations. I had to keep reminding myself he was insane.

"You're free to go any time you feel up to the journey. I wouldn't recommend it until I'm satisfied you won't relapse anytime soon. Your horse is in good hands—you may examine it whenever you like, it's a splendid animal—and I'll provide you with directions to Cabo Falso. It would be ungrateful of me to reward you for the gift of the *Ghost* by making you a prisoner."

"And Joseph?"

"He'll follow—once he's instructed my men in the operation of the locomotive."

He read my thoughts. "No, I wouldn't charge these creatures with anything more complex than cutting cane. You've yet to meet the rest of my regulars. McCready trained the men under his direct command, and I trained him.

"You'll find your other things in the cabinet. Ysabel has cleaned and pressed them by now. You'll be more comfortable once you're out of these rags."

As he spoke, he patted the pocket containing the Gatling round.

I left him in his private study, cracking open a book the size and apparent weight of a paving stone, and entered the bedroom, well-lit now with a similar set of heavy green curtains spread on either side of a window as tall as the others. A scuttle-shaped iron bathtub, lined with white porcelain, steamed in the middle of the rug I'd stepped on earlier. If it had been there in the dark I'd have bumped into it, so Ysabel—if that was the Yaqui woman who'd served coffee—would have had to enlist a couple of Childress' trained monkeys to carry it in; those gnarled hands of hers would have found challenge enough lugging in buckets of scalding water. I'd been bathed repeatedly, I supposed, but although the heat was moderate that far above sea level, my skin glistened greasily once I'd stripped. Whatever effect Childress' justice had or hadn't had on its audience, it was enough to break me into a sweat even if I'd been in the midst of a winter in Montana Territory.

I took the cartridge out of the pocket of the coat, hefted it, and tossed it into a corner. I hadn't the slightest idea what use I might make of it, apart from the fact it was the one secret I'd managed to retain. His knowing it robbed it of all value. I'd gone up against men before who were smarter than I was, more ruthless, readier to act when the moment presented itself; this was the first time I found myself face-to-face with a man who embodied all three—

Virtues? Make of it what you like. One or the other or the other yet had seen me to a ripe old age in my work.

The painting I'd glimpsed in the gloom wasn't much less murky in broad daylight. It was smaller than I'd thought—the heavy filigreed frame almost overwhelmed it—and darkened with age and layers of dirt, cheap varnish laid in over dirt, and more dirt laid in over the varnish, but it seemed to show a man bound in the rags of what must once have been grand martial attire, being disemboweled by a band of curly-haired men in some kind of peasant dress. There appeared to be a signature in the lower right-hand corner, illegible under the layers of grime and shellac. A ghastly thing, probably worth a lot of money to people in New York and St. Louis.

The clothes I'd packed, with some exceptions I noted later, were folded and hung in the cedar cabinet, with my range hat and the fawn-colored Montana pinch I wore to special occasions sharing the top shelf. There was no sign of the overalls and flannel shirt I'd borrowed from Joseph to wear while serving as fireman; Childress had been student enough of human behavior to separate them from my personality. He'd studied me as surely as his poets and philosophers. I suspected I had Felix Bonaparte, the Alamos attorney, to thank for supplying him with information. He'd be Childress' conduit to the greater world.

That thought nudged me in the ribs, painfully enough to hurt, but not enough to tell me why. I'd been threatened, shot at, shot almost through, weakened with plague, and stood to witness cold-blooded murder masquerading as execution. You don't count that kind of time in hours or days or weeks or years; centuries hardly answered. I'd forgotten everything about my meeting with Bonaparte apart from the man himself and his oily command of English.

I lowered myself into the tub gingerly, gasping with each inch, but the sensation of being parboiled melded into a deceptive feeling of well-being as the heat penetrated bruised muscles and strained tendons. Compared to the tarry yellow soap I'd been used to in boarding houses and railroad hotels, the cake in the dish, lavender-scented and impressed with an escutcheon of some kind, wouldn't have turned up the nose of Queen Victoria.

Lathering up, I noted for the first time that my injured hand had been re-bandaged with the same attention paid to my scalp. I attributed that to the woman as well; but I was as wrong about that as I was about the house being an illusion and the gourds that turned out to be skulls. After I'd dried myself with a towel as thick and soft as any to be found in the best hotels in Denver, I picked up the German book on the nightstand and found it dog-eared to a page with pen-and-ink illustrations detailing the process of cleansing and dressing open wounds, with whole paragraphs of text underscored in ink fresh enough to still carry a scent. A Mexican squaw might be able to interpret the drawings, but it seemed unlikely she'd read German, with Latin phrases interlaced, much less select passages for closer study.

Something else shared the nightstand: A sepia photograph in a silver frame of a pleasant-faced woman bombazined to the neck, the collar closed with the standard cameo brooch, with her hair skinned back into what would be a tight bun and—I couldn't shake the certainty—the devil's own time trying to appear grave for the man behind the camera; she seemed about to burst into laughter. This, I thought, would be the fiancée Childress had left in Virginia. Naked as I was, I slapped nonexistent pockets for the packet of letters I'd been given by lawyer Bonaparte.

I had it then, the most important part of our conversation; which is always the first to go under pressure. Bonaparte had given me the packet for delivery, and it had weighed less heavily in my pocket than the useless piece of ammunition Childress had known about all along.

He surely had the letters by now, if the walking corpses who'd brought me up the mountain hadn't burned them for kindling; or used them even less respectably.

I made a decision not to bring up the subject. If the wretches had mistreated the letters in their childish ignorance and he found out, there would be at least one more head on a pole, and another decapitated body on his utilitarian pile.

Why I should think any more of them than of a stag whose head might decorate the wall of some gentlemen's club, or a prize-winning bass mounted on a board in a saloon, eluded me; unless it was the conviction that, generations back, a normal woman had lain with a normal man, with no thought beyond creating a normal family, human at least. What had come from that was no one's fault; unless you embraced the existence of Satan.

Which I surely did. A man could not have seen what I'd seen, met whom I'd met, and still denied it. Tidy dress and a broad knowledge of science, literature, and the arts were cover enough for horns and a tail.

For some reason I couldn't recall, I'd packed a fine linen shirt I'd had made to my measure in San Francisco, and the suit of clothes I wore to make a good impression testifying in Judge Blackthorne's court. Maybe I thought I'd be invited to a state dinner in the governor's palace in Mexico City upon the successful completion of my mission. Someone had brushed the suit to a sheen. That the valise containing this finery had been carried up the mountain with greater care than my engineer, said something about the character of my escort; but I didn't dwell on that. The clothes, and a fresh set of cotton underdrawers, were laid out on the turned-down bed as if by a valet. On the floor at the foot of the bed stood my second-best pair of boots—I'd left the best behind to be resoled—blacked and buffed to a mirror finish. Oscar Childress, it appeared, was gearing up for diplomatic occasions, accustoming himself to entertaining elegant guests.

Well, what was so ludicrous about that? I hadn't much history compared to my host's, but if I'd never read beyond the Bible I'd still know that being mad has never posed much of a drawback to ruling a nation.

TWENTY-SIX

The old Mexican woman knocked at the door while I was putting on my shirt. I let her in carrying a tray containing a pitcher of hot water, a fresh folded white towel, a pearl-handled razor, and another cake of the lavender-scented soap in a silver mug.

A plain tin mirror hung on a nail above a washstand next to the window. Leaving my shirt open, I filled the basin and scraped off the growth of weeks, the Spanish steel blade gliding through the coarse stubble like a scythe through corn silk. After rinsing off, I slapped on bay rum from a flask on the stand and stared at the stranger in the mirror. I'd begun to resemble Childress' creatures, but shiny-faced and clean-smelling in my best clothes I might pass muster in the drawing-room of a Forty-Niner; if he hadn't become so rich he'd forgotten his time grubbing in gulches and riverbeds and sharing his tent with lice and rats the size of cocker spaniels.

I went into the study, but it was deserted. Retracing our path to the front porch, I found my host seated in a spring buggy with a sleek rubber top hitched to a deep-bellied black with one white stocking and blinders, a rig straight out of Montgomery Ward. He wore an ankle-length duster over his indoor clothes and a milk-white straw planter's hat with a wagon-wheel brim and a black silk band. Outside the shelter of the porch roof, his face was dishwater gray, the black's reins wrapped around wrists thin as drawn gold. In those surroundings he might have passed for a missionary with an unmentionable disease, exiled to the wilderness to die.

He'd stopped beside the blue enamel mounting-block, but although it glistened from a fresh scrubbing I avoided it as I stepped aboard and sat beside him on the upholstered leather seat.

"How far are we going?"

"No more than a thousand yards; but as it's all uphill I wouldn't recommend it for strolling. Every month or so one of the poor idiots stumbles and drops off the edge." He shook the reins and we started forward.

A ledge wound around the mountain nearest the house like the screw on a printer's press, railed with stretches of pine on the outside. Where there wasn't a horizontal surface sufficient to support them, the land fell nearly perpendicular from the edge. In places the path was just wide enough for the wheels to maintain a purchase, with pebbles and broken shards squirting out from under them and caroming down the mountainside. It had in the solider patches a finished look of black stone, not at all the rough fluting caused by centuries of erosion. I said it looked like a proper road.

"It's a road; though I'd hesitate to apply the honorific. We started with dynamite, but we had to conserve it for more practical use, as the supply lines are long and the merchants are vultures. Also, there's brittle shale tucked in between the veins of granite. I lost a fine engineer to a landslide. When the creatures came along I was able to free the men of skill for worthier work."

As he said it, we passed a crew of his creatures dismantling a cairn of fallen stone with picks and spades. Stripped to the waist, they were all bunched raw muscle, indistinguishable from the mountain itself until they moved or the sun glistened off their sweat. At sight of the buggy, they shouldered their tools and flattened themselves against the rock while we passed within inches, sending a shower of dislodged mountain tumbling. I gripped the vehicle's white-ash frame tight enough to split the skin of my knuckles, leaning against the driver like an infatuated maiden out for a turn in the park.

"The brutes are good for something," he said. "What they lack in brain power they more than make up for in animal strength, and they can survive for a week trapped under a ton of rubble."

"How frequent are the slides?"

"Constant. Most of them are minor, but there are days when I'm unable to visit the plantation. The Sierras never miss an opportunity to reclaim what's been taken from them."

At length the ground leveled off, until we came to a plane several acres large, so flat it seemed something had lopped off the top of the mountain the way the machete had decapitated the poor creature before the house. Long buildings of log resembled military barracks, and there were two large constructions of stone standing against a curtain of cane, the stalks growing as high as ten feet, with half-naked creatures plowing aisles through the thick growth with truncated blades, swinging them like sickles. Others gathered the mown stalks and threw them into the beds of wagons hitched to mules and oxen. The crunch of the falling cane and the swish of the bundles as they were piled into heaps sounded like an eighty-mile-an-hour wind leveling a forest.

We alighted from the buggy, and Childress' place was taken by a white man in a butternut uniform, patched and darned all over, who saluted him smartly. He was the first probable member of the major's original command I'd seen apart from Captain McCready. He drove the buggy around the corner of one of the stone buildings.

"I was told so many times that sugar won't grow at this altitude I began to believe it." Childress was shouting over the din. "I've since formed the opinion that the big interests had their eye on the place and sought to discourage competition. As a rule, cane grows to eight feet, sometimes nine; but as you can see, the climate and conditions are ideal, and possibly unique. I provide most of the sugar sold in Acapulco, and since I began marketing in Mexico City, the Cuban interests have petitioned the government to enjoin any United States citizen from participating in the trade. Since I'm the only one in the business, I find that complimentary in the extreme."

"Why would a rich man want to conquer a nation?"

When he scowled, the paper-thin skin plastered to his skull broke into a myriad of wrinkles.

"Money is only a means to power. Any man who would settle for the first is no better than a carpetbagger."

He pulled open a heavy door, gripping the iron handle with both hands, and we entered one of the stone buildings. When he shut the door behind us, the cacophony outside ceased. The interior was as big as a warehouse on the docks of San Francisco, lit by sunlight canting through mullioned windows just under the rafters, fifteen feet above our heads. Plank catwalks suspended by thick ropes circled the walls and bisected one another in tiers, with more laborers stripped to the waist standing and walking along them, supporting themselves on the hemp rails.

The top tier was occupied entirely by men in Confederate uniform carrying rifles. He saw me looking at them.

"No, they're not enforced labor. They're fed, sheltered, and all their medical needs are addressed, far better than when they were trying to survive on their own. Their tempers are quicker than their powers of reason: An accidental collision is seldom shrugged off, and once engaged, they fight to the death unless someone stops them."

"Shoots them, you mean."

"It rarely comes to that. As I said, their senses are unnaturally acute. The report alone is agony to their ears, and a near-miss is sufficient to distract them. Their ability to maintain their purpose is almost nonexistent. They literally forget what sparked the fight, or that they were fighting at all. Repetitive work like cutting cane and pulling ropes is more suited to them than anything they might attempt through any will of their own.

"I won't show you the other building," he said; "to do so would be redundant, and the heat is miserable. There the cane is mashed into a pulp, boiled in copper cauldrons, and distilled. It liquefies at a temperature of one hundred sixty degrees. I don't know how the brutes stand it. Before I discovered them, the men I employed had to work in shifts no longer than fifteen minutes. We lost three in one month when they weakened and fell into the cauldrons, ruining half a day's output. Here is where the final refinement process takes place."

A waterfall of golden syrupy liquid gushed from a wooden vat tilted on ropes and pulleys into a larger container, filled nearly to the top with black ash and erected on a platform in the center of the hardpack floor. A sluice, wooden also, slanted down from the base of the larger vat into another on the floor, where the liquid came out as clear as water. The air was filled with a stench like scorched hair and the heavier, almost seductive smell of molasses.

"Charcoal." Childress pointed to the contents of the larger vat. "We fire it in kilns from bone, grind it fine in revolving barrels, much like gunpowder, and pour the juice through it, leaving the impurities behind."

I made no response, knowing the source of the bone.

"We let the liquid cool and crystallize in clay vessels. What moisture remains is then spun out of it in more rotating barrels by centrifugal force. The pulverizing itself is by mortar and pestle, albeit it on a grander scale than ordinary."

He turned to face me. "And that, Marshal, is how you manage to take the bitterness out of your coffee."

We went back outside, where the noise of cutting and stacking was as loud as before. Strolling toward the stalks of cane, I peered between the rows.

Childress missed nothing. "Don't strain your eyes looking for the poppies. They're indistinguishable from common weeds when they're not in bloom. In any case I'm phasing out the trade in opium. The refining process is even more elaborate than sugar and the market is limited to those who can afford it. I can move the legitimate product in much greater volume, without fear of confiscation except by the locals, who are cheap to bribe.

"You wouldn't credit it," he said, "but the world's addiction to sugar far surpasses all the others. Any country practitioner can furnish you with laudanum, but men have slain each other over a peppermint stick. If I'd never touched a gram of opium, I doubt you'd have been sent here. A rebellion without financing is only the pipe-dream of a lunatic, but more governments have been overturned on traffic in harmless indulgences than drugs; but try running for re-election on bananas and tobacco."

"What's in the other buildings, besides the barracks and infirmary?"

"The women's quarters; brothel, seraglio, call it what you will. Simple creatures require simple pleasures. The brutes fight over them as much as over anything else, but if I'd left them behind they'd be buggering each other all the time, and I can't have that. Whatever else you may think of me, I am a southern gentleman."

Two flags flew atop the nearest barracks, the stars-and-bars of the Confederacy and the other bearing the visored and laurel-encircled head of the Knights of the Golden Circle. A stable had been built onto the end of the structure, as long as the barracks itself and lined with stalls on both sides. Here one of Childress' creatures was at work shoveling manure into a great pile outside the back entrance, and more well-tended mounts, each branded CSA, blew and twitched their tails at flies. My bay occupied a stall at the end, looking no worse the wear for its journey in the stock car.

Childress' horse and buggy waited for us outside the stable, with the soldier who'd driven it holding it by the bit. He saluted as his commander grasped the frame and started to pull himself into the driver's seat.

His hand lost its grip and he folded slowly to the ground, like a barn collapsing. The soldier lunged forward and stooped to help him up, but he was as limp as the dead creature the others had slung onto the bonepile, his face even grayer than before. Major Oscar Childress, the southern gentleman who owned slaves, sold poison, ran whores, and conspired in treason, was close to death.

TWENTY-SEVEN

Childress, I decided, was never far outside the scrutiny of his subordinates. No sooner had the soldier lifted him from the ground than Captain McCready appeared, straddling his fine sorrel, and swung down from the saddle in one fluid movement. He took the fallen man by the shoulders, the other by the ankles, and together they carried him to the next barracks over. I followed, leaving Childress' straw hat where it had landed.

The room they took him to was small and separated from the rest of the building with a pine partition, scoured white and stinking of carbolic. A hospital bed erected on a system of cranks and wheels stood in the center of the room, made up in fresh linen, with two down pillows and a thick cotton blanket rolled up at the foot in a topsheet. In seconds they had the patient laid out with the covers drawn to his chin. Dismissed, the soldier evaporated; there's no better way to describe how quickly he made himself absent.

There was an evil smell about the place I knew all too well, apart from the carbolic: the thick air of ether, old blood, rotting flesh, and alcohol; gallons of the last, splashed about like water on a raging fire, and over it all the gaseous residue of human organs exposed to the air. It brought me back to a place and a time I'd hoped was long behind me; of a mildewed tent in a farmer's decimated field packed with sweating, cursing orderlies, frantic surgeons, and grown men screaming for their mothers. The farther you got away from a thing the closer you came back to it.

"Lift his head."

There being no one else present, I slid a hand behind Childress' head and raised it while the captain opened a shallow drawer in a cabinet with a zinc top and took out a red morocco case the thickness of a deck of cards but twice as long. Tipping back the lid, he drew a steel syringe from its form-fitted depression, a squat brown bottle from another, shook the bottle, drew the cork, and filled the syringe with a sucking sound. He restopped and replaced the bottle, tapped the barrel of the syringe, depressed the plunger, squirting an arc of liquid from the end of the hollow needle, and in a series of deft motions wetted a wad of cotton from another container he'd taken from the drawer, tipped something from another bottle into the wad, and cocked an elbow, pointing at his superior's near arm with an unmistakable gesture.

Unmistakable for only a few.

How he knew I'd filled in for a stricken orderly at Cold Harbor I never learned; either he'd studied my record or expected me to understand what must have been an automatic action. Whichever was the case, he'd judged correctly. I rolled back Childress' sleeve and watched as he daubed the inside of the major's elbow with the cotton swab, filling the room with the sharp stench of alcohol, cast the swab to the floor, pierced the vein he knew was there, and made the injection.

"Opium?" I asked.

"Highly distilled," he said. "One of the major's discoveries. I don't pretend to know how it works, only that it does."

I watched Childress' face, gray as dead clay. He'd been breathing shallowly, in short bursts. As the medicine took hold, his lungs filled, then emptied, and fell afterward into the rhythm of a man in deep slumber.

All the paraphernalia was returned to its place in the same measured order as it had been brought into play. McCready cocked his head to bring his one eye to the operation. I saw then that the dead socket wasn't empty after all: Worm-shaped muscles pulsed as if they were still in charge of a working orb.

"I know a glass-blower in Helena who could fit you with an eye no one would notice," I said. "A U.S. senator came all the way from Washington on his reputation."

"I tried that. A fellow from someplace called Vienna had one painted from a chip he matched to the eye God gave me. Beautiful thing. I keep it in the case it came with." He shook his head. "Too much time had passed. The skin had shriveled too far to support it. It kept popping out at inopportune times. Better the truth up front than to have the lie exposed over a plate of oysters in champagne sauce."

He smiled then; anyway the wide, thin-lipped mouth in the piebald face twitched at the corners. I felt a twinge of respect, for the soldier if not for the executioner. We might have faced each other across a battlefield strewn with men we'd both murdered for no reason I could remember, but loyalty is rare even in civilization.

"What's his complaint?"

"He's being eaten from inside; it's this blasted climate, and his own genius consuming itself in the company of idiots. It hasn't gotten to his brain, that much is certain. That's the hell of it. Those brutes next door, dying of their own sinful birth, don't know what's happening to them, and are all the better for it."

As if in response, a guttural cry arose from one of the adjacent rooms. If it had been at least half-animal I could have put it aside; that it was more than half-human was impossible to ignore.

McCready was an educated man, that much was certain. The southern universities had it all over the ivy leagues of the North. Their founders had come straight from Oxford and Cambridge.

"How long does he have?" I asked.

"He went to see a specialist in El Paso. Crossing the border could have meant his life, but I suppose he found that preferable to this. The doctor could have practiced in Chicago or Denver, maybe even New York City, but he was loyal to the War for Southern Independence, and couldn't countenance treating Yankees. He estimated six months. That was a year and a half ago. The major rebels against everything." He stuck out his hand. "Eustace McCready, Captain of the Confederacy."

I gripped the hand as firmly as I could. It was like taking hold of a train coupling. "Page Murdock, Corporal of the Union."

The mouth parted, exposing a fine set of coral-colored teeth: He seemed to know his wine. "I started as a corporal with the Chesterfield Volunteers."

A division I was unfamiliar with; but then Childress had assembled his own regiment from among the oldest families in Virginia. "My mistake," I said. "I wasn't aware you'd worked for a living."

He made a sound I took for amusement. We were close comrades, for that moment at least; and in silence agreed how sorry we'd be when one of us killed the other.

He pried apart Childress' eyelids, striking a match off a thumbnail to study the pupils. "He'll rest for a day. With God's good grace he'll come out of it roaring for someone's head. I don't envy the first of these brutes who fall beneath his expectations."

"Well, you need the bones."

McCready straightened to his full height, easily a head above mine, and fixed me with his eye, blue-green and as clear as egg-whites around the irises.

"He doesn't need the excuse. This country is as rich in game as the one you came from, before the blasted federals raped it of buffalo to bring the Indians to their knees. That grizzly the brutes slew and dragged across the tracks will be harvested and put to good use. What does it serve to set aside the bones of these creatures—or you, or me, comes to that—to waste in graves? If we truly believed in life hereafter, there would be no reason to visit a cemetery. I'd rather my remains be put to use than moldering six feet under. The uncivilized peoples of the East believe that death is not final, only rebirth. Who is to say I won't someday sweeten the tea of a saint?"

"Or of a St. Louis whore; you don't have a vote. You're just coughing up something your worshipful master said over a dinner table."

"And who do you serve, that fat New York Yankee in the White House?"

"Is that who's in? I haven't voted since Abe Lincoln."

"That carpetbagger?"

I looked around the room. Apart from another finely woven rug, it was undecorated except for a small painting in a heavy frame: Another murky representation of coarsely dressed peasants, this time gouging the eyes out of another captive in the rags of a fine uniform. I made some comment about his commander's taste in art.

McCready's eyes jerked toward the painting. "He buys those at auction, by wire. I don't see much difference between them and Antietam."

"He wants to bring it all back," I said. "If you really want to know who I'm serving, it's anyone who stands in front of that."

Just then the soldier he'd dismissed entered. I saw from his unlined face, the chin pale of any trace of shaved whiskers, that he was too young to have served Childress in combat. The generation that had come up since the war had been all too ready to offer its services to the glamour of a lost cause.

McCready returned his salute. "What?"

"Sir. The men are wondering."

"*Wondering?*" He pronounced the word as if it belonged to a foreign language.

The young man cleared his throat; if anyone had ever wanted to be somewhere else, this was him. "In the absence of the major, are the maneuvers to proceed as always?"

The captain inhaled and exhaled, a mighty gust. "Look you, private. Who is the man in this bed?"

To his credit, the private didn't look. "Major Childress, sir."

"Is he absent?"

"No, sir!" Had the young man straightened further, his spine would have cracked.

"Then go to the devil with you, and look smart during the maneuvers."

"Yes, sir!"

McCready deflated a little after the man's exit. "If this is what we have to work with, so be it. The major will whip them into shape."

Just then the major drew a mighty breath. His eyes opened, exposing the bright orbs, blazing now, like dying suns: the same fierce fire that had come through at Cold Harbor and Bull Run. We both leaned in to hear his gasp:

"God forgive me."

He'd taken in too much breath for the purpose; the rest went out in a gush of air. It was his last.

TWENTY-EIGHT

When great men die, they say, the room in which they expired always seems larger; as if the soul that had passed from it had filled it to the walls.

Oscar Childress' death-room didn't look or feel any different from when he'd been brought there, his heart still beating, feeding that singular brain. The man himself seemed smaller; but even dolts shrivel a bit when the life-force has departed.

He lay with his eyes open—less bright by the moment—and his lips still parted just enough to let his last three words escape. He'd have hated them, I was sure. He had to have known his time was near, and thought to draft a valedictory worthy of a giant; but even a gifted actor can forget his lines in a role more challenging than the rest. *God forgive me*: a plea so banal as to be worthy of any of his brainless creatures.

McCready—inspired, perhaps, by his commander's triteness at the finish—performed the conventional duties, kneading shut his eyes and tipping the jaw closed. Comically, it dropped back open, forcing him to repeat the operation and hold it for a moment like a cabinetmaker clamping two pieces of wood together until the glue set. From Moses to Alexander to Washington, and all the saints and generals who had come before and between and after, the epilogue would have proceeded similarly, with a lesser light sweeping up the ashes of the extinguished blaze. I left then. He'd forgotten about me, and would hold that position until the dead muscles went rigid, if that was what it took.

The infirmary was built on the shotgun plan, with the rooms connected end-to-end like railroad cars. I went through a door, crossed a vacant room with the mattress rolled up against a plain iron headboard, and entered the next. There lay Joseph, on his back with a thin blanket drawn to his bare chest and his hands folded on top of it. I stood watching for several seconds before I confirmed his chest was rising and falling. His eyes didn't open and I chose not to wake him. There was a forest of brown bottles on a plain table beside the bed, some with rubber droppers. The air was strong with a sharp smell I'd grown accustomed to lately: the fumes from the juice distilled from cinchona bark, Mexico's answer to malaria. I took myself back out.

The captain was still standing beside Childress' bed, with his chin on his chest and his hands crossed at his waist. Whether he was praying silently or waiting for his master to rise from the dead I couldn't say; more likely for a military man he was considering the next move. I left, making as little noise as possible. He seemed to have forgotten I existed, which was how I would have had it.

There was no sign of my saddle or bridle in the stables. Likely it had been left aboard the *Ghost* when my bay was hitched to one of the wagons. I outfitted it with the tack available and picked my way back down the trail, dismounting and leading it when the way narrowed and an attack of malaria might throw off my balance at any minute. The creatures clearing away fallen debris went on working as I passed; without Childress along, I might have been a bird pecking for grubs in cracks for all I was visible to them.

Nearing the house I passed the cannon I'd heard earlier, a blue-black six-pounder Napoleon mounted on wheels as tall as a man, stinking, like the dead grizzly, of rancid fat greasing the barrel and also the sulphur stench of burnt cordite, and here and there a soldier on foot or on horseback, their uniforms tidy but as patched and darned as ancient quilts. Once again, I attracted little attention. I could have pranced around in the arrogant scarlet of a Yankee Zouave and drawn no more than a sneer. In an armed camp, much is taken for granted.

"Major Childress is dead."

The captain's drill-trained voice rang without emotion; he must have finished tidying up just after I left and ridden straight back to the barn. A contingent of men wearing uniforms in varying degrees of repair would be gathered in formation before the house, with their immediate commander standing at parade rest on the front porch. There would be a general removal of hats.

Apart from the announcement itself, which reached me in Childress' study, I assumed the scene had played out as described; I'd only heard the bugle call to Assembly and the jingling of raiments and sabers.

The key was missing from the lock, but I rolled the desk

chair across the room and tilted it, jamming the back under the knob. I wished it hadn't had casters; a strong shove would clear the path inside, but it would slow an intruder down for a second or two.

The room was as the major had left it, with the enormous book he'd been reading still flayed open on the desk; a thing of stiff heavy leaves unevenly cut and decorated with pen-and-ink illustrations tinted by a hand that had been skeletal for at least two centuries, lettered elaborately in a language I will never know; from the charted coastlines and studies of animals I recognized as pumas and buffalo despite their exaggerated features, it seemed to be a tract on the New World based on early French explorations; in all likelihood his talk of monsters on the map had prompted him to crack it. The pipe he'd smoked while reading, carved from ivory (or what I hoped was ivory) into the likeness of a horned creature with an amber stem, lay still warm in an onyx bowl, permeating the room further with its rich fragrance.

Another smell, coarser and acidic, drew my attention to the parlor stove and to its door, which was slightly ajar. I took it by its dangling coiled handle, tipped it open, drew a short poker from the brass rack beside the stove, and separated the ashes, which had gone out but for a few sparks that erupted into vertical threads of flame when I disturbed them. A bit of charred cloth came apart from a thick sheaf of burned paper, which itself separated in two sections, exposing under it an image impressed on stiff cardboard curved at the corners. A hole had burned through the center, obliterating the face, but the flames had cast a rose hue on what was left of a high-collared dress—bombazine, beyond doubt. I felt no need to go into the room where I'd slept to confirm that he'd taken the photograph from the silver frame on the nightstand and burned it along with the letters the woman had written to him. He hadn't even bothered to untie the ribbon, much less read them. I'd fretted for nothing over whether they'd reached him and what might happen to his creatures if they'd failed to deliver them.

I remembered Childress' notes on his report to the American authorities, and the possibly mistranslated suggestion to "plant seeds" (*matea*) among the unsophisticated natives of Mexico to foster their awestruck regard for their neighbors to the North America: What he'd actually written was *mata*: "kill." The error had not been his. A man who would exterminate the creatures, as he had been doing piecemeal on the pretext of setting an example to the others, would destroy every link to the civilized life he'd known in Virginia.

For months or years, he'd slept beside that likeness, until it occupied his thoughts no more (or not as much) as his paintings of fierce peasants torturing prisoners of war to death, until the letters came to remind him. Then he'd thrown the photograph in the fire with the lot.

I went back to the desk. The belly drawer was unlocked, but there was nothing of interest in it. The same was true of five of the six deeper drawers that flanked the kneehole. The last I tried was locked. I'd seen nothing resembling a key, but took a silver-plated paper knife from the blotter and poked it this way and that inside the keyhole, tugging on the bronze lion's-head knob, until something snapped and the drawer came open.

The first thing that greeted me was my old Deane-Adams in its gun belt. I inspected the cylinder, found all the chambers loaded, and buckled the rig around my waist. I looked for the Bulldog revolver, without success; but I hadn't had it nearly as long and was less familiar with it, so I didn't spend much time regretting the loss.

On the bottom of the drawer lay a black iron strong box

edged with gilded oak leaves. It, too, was locked, but I inserted the scratched paper knife under the lid and forced it open.

Some of the papers inside were in Latin. These I set aside. At the bottom was a long parchment envelope sealed with the K.G.C. crest impressed in red wax. I broke it open and unfolded the parchment sheets from inside. It was lettered in copperplate and signed by Childress.

I skimmed through the bequests; for it bore all the highblown obsolete language of a will. There was no mention of his fiancée's name, and I recognized none of the others. Upon the signer's passing, command of the army was to pass to Eustace McCready, Captain (to be promoted to the brevet rank of major upon acceptance). On the fourth page was the passage I'd been looking for:

> *Under no circumstances is my death or incapacity to interfere with the purpose of this militia, which is to march upon Mexico City and by military engagement induce the government of Mexico to surrender the command of its forces to Captain McCready, who will annex them to the militia and invade the United States of America.*

A sound outside brought me to my feet; it was the clank of a dangling saber in its metal scabbard banging against a boottop. Either Captain McCready or one of his subordinates was coming to gather the personal effects of their deceased leader or was looking for me.

I refolded the sheets and put them in the inside pocket of my coat.

My way was clear. If my suspicions were right and I had been allowed to live only because Childress wanted fresh conversation, my usefulness was at an end. Unless McCready disobeyed the posthumous command—and if anything the man would be even more fanatically devoted to the major now than when he breathed, he'd be more interested in taking possession of the *Ghost,* in which case Joseph the engineer's existence was more secure than my own. The Indian had saved my life, but he was in no condition to escape that place, and from what I'd seen of the infirmary his chances were better there than anywhere within a hundred miles.

But a hundred miles from where? I had no idea how far I'd been brought from the train, or in which direction other than up. To miss it by fifty yards in either direction would be the same as missing it entirely. I could wander along the rails for days, then blunder into an ambush; or break my neck riding down a grade as steep as a grain elevator in search of a fly-speck on the map called Cabo Falso.

Map.

The saber was jangling down the hallway. I spotted the ancient Spanish wall decoration in its frame. I took along the paper knife and slashed the map all around the inside edge. The doorknob rattled, someone pushed at the door, encountered the resistance of the chair. Whoever it was put his shoulder into it. The chair's wheels skidded out from under it and it fell on its back. It bought me a second.

I bought another. A slug from the Deane-Adams split a heavy panel. I hadn't hoped to hit anything, just play for time. I loped to the connecting door to the bedroom.

The key was in the lock. I turned it and swung open the door just in time to stop a slug from the man who'd pushed in from the hall. Just as I jerked the door shut, I caught a glimpse of a gaping eye socket in a face black with fury.

TWENTY-NINE

The room where I'd recovered was a bedroom once again, with no sign of the bathtub or shaving materials; the late Major Childress had run a tight ship in a country not notorious for its discipline. I'd brought the key inside with me and turned it in the lock just as a hand grasped the knob on the other side, and got away from the door an instant ahead of the next bullet. This one penetrated the thick pine and punched a hole in the tall window across from it.

I didn't waste time returning fire. In another moment the lock would be shot off or the door forced. I snatched up the heavy washstand and flung it that direction, but I didn't look to see if it fell to the floor in a position to slow down pursuit. That kind of time goes for gold double-eagles, and I hadn't a penny to spare. I crumpled up the ancient map and stuffed it into a pocket on the run.

The window was the only other way out. I used the barrel of

my revolver to clear away the rest of the glass and got a leg over the sill just as the crash came, accompanied by splintering wood. For good measure I slung another piece of lead that direction and dropped four feet to the ground.

Or to be more exact, onto a pile of skeletons. At that corner of the house they reached to the sill.

There was no getting through that grotesque stack except the long way. The closest end, at the rear of the house, led to a cliff that fell hundreds of feet almost straight down the mountain. I'd climbed and descended as bad in like situations, but not when I was still recovering from serious illness, with the possibility of a fresh attack coming on while I was hanging by my fingers from a slippery shelf of rock. Even if I made it to level ground, I'd be on foot in country I didn't know and easily recaptured. I'd left my bay tethered to the rail of the front porch.

So on I went, stumbling over rib cages, flinging aside skulls and pelvises and arms angled like cranes. Stiff jagged fingers snagged my coat and snatched at my hat as if they were the last to give up. Razor-sharp sternums slashed at my shins. I tripped and fell, shouting, into grisly spirals of bone, struggled in a panic to untangle myself from limbs I swore still had life in them. There was more than dried stalks in that heap; it had been added to as recently as that morning, and I breathed through my mouth to avoid the stench when I wasn't gritting my teeth against the likelihood of sinking my fingers into rotting remains. Flies the size of hummingbirds floated on the foul air, buzzing drunkenly, their abdomens glistening emerald-green. They landed on my face, favoring the moist corners of my mouth and eyes, and quitted with sullen reluctance when I swiped at them. They flew so slowly, fattened on their feast, I caught three of them in mid-air, only half-trying, and batted them to the ground. All around me sections of human jetsam plinked and plunked and clattered like someone striking together hollow sticks for the pure perverse pleasure of making a racket.

The same thing was happening behind me, as McCready came hard on my heels.

A bullet screamed a foot past my ear and crackled to a stop in a nest of bones. I didn't stop, and when he heard the noise he returned to the chase. I'd gained ground while he stopped to level his pistol.

My luck held. I made my way through that charnel yard without encountering putrefying flesh, and stumbled into the open.

My luck didn't hold. My bay wasn't where I'd left it.

No, it still held. When I raced around the end of the porch, it was standing nearer the front door; I'd been careless with the tether, leaving enough slack for the animal to drag it down toward an inviting clump of grass.

That was where my luck gave out. A group of men dressed in rags with pinched-in heads stood at the far end of the house facing me, their eyes dull between sunken temples, but their unsheathed machetes burning bright in the sun.

I didn't want to do it. The wretches were little more than the brutes Childress had called them, but human, and hardly in command of their lives. They existed because of Childress and for Childress; they knew no other god. When the first one lumbered toward me, raising his short-bladed weapon, I shot a fresh hole in the crown of his hat high up, snatching it off his low cranium. I might have been shooting at the house for all the effect it had. He took another stumbling step, swinging the machete back as far as his arm would reach. Cracked lips skinned back from black gums, spittle bubbling in the corners.

I aimed lower and fired. He was still coming when the scarlet stain spread all the way across his belly; then he tripped over his own feet and fell headlong, landing stiff as a plank with his weapon still at arm's length, and lay without jerking so much as a nerve.

By then the others were on the move. If, as the major had said, they understood only fear and hatred, the second was stronger than the first. I didn't think they mourned their comrade so much as saw me for a member of an alien tribe, where wrath and fear intermingled, like grease and fire, leading to white flame. It hardly seemed possible the news of Childress' death had reached them, but if their instincts were as bestial as he'd made them out to be, they might have smelled it, the way they said some breeds of dog can detect disease before a trained physician can suspect it. In any case his order to spare me from harm was no longer regarded.

I could have shot them all. It was a small group, and their reflexes were so primitive it would have been like picking bottles off a fence rail, but maybe because of that I saw no honor in it, even in defense of my own life. When the first of the rest came within blade's reach I swept the barrel of the revolver against his wrist, where the bone was as obvious as those in the pile I'd struggled my way through, and striking it with a noise that was half-thump, half-crack. He yelped and stumbled, losing his grip on his weapon, and I followed through, shoving him off his feet with my forearm.

By then I had my hand on the bay's reins, but as I jerked them loose of the rail a vise closed on my gun arm just above the elbow. It went dead to the shoulder and I felt the butt slipping through my fingers. The creature could have cracked a cue ball in that fist. Something flashed in the sun; I threw up my other arm, expecting the blade to slash through muscle and tendon as easily as it sliced cane; but something struck with a thud and a third eye opened at the bridge of his nose. The machete spun out of his hand, hitting my shoulder with the flat of the blade and bouncing off. He fell even faster than his partner; those weak minds had only a tenuous connection to their bodies, and switched off like a telegraph key snatched loose of its wires.

I heard the echo of the shot then, but I didn't sacrifice a second looking over my shoulder to confirm it was McCready who'd fired. I swung the bay between me and his weapon, hooked one foot over the edge of the saddle, and loosed a round close enough to its ear to put it to gallop. We took off toward the mountain trail I'd come up by wagon, I riding Apache fashion, hanging on by a handful of mane with one foot lifted just short of the ground and the horse serving as a moving breastwork shielding me from lead.

Not that it stopped the captain, who seemed to have no more sentiment for the beast than I; a bullet struck the saddle-horn square, gouging the leather and ricocheting off the hickory core, and when I had the opportunity later to examine the bay's hindquarters I saw where another had plowed a furrow a half-inch deep through the flesh behind the cantle.

Which would have been the moment when the animal screamed and took off like Pegasus.

I wouldn't repeat that ride. The way down from the house to where we'd left the train was as steep as the way up from it to the plantation, but I'd made both trips aboard the relative safety of a wheeled vehicle under someone's control. Just galloping on flat ground plugged my throat with my heart, and I don't trust the animal at even a slow walk.

More shots came, rattling and growing fainter. When they stopped—to reload, I thought—I swung my leg across the saddle and pulled myself upright, and almost as an afterthought holstered the Deane-Adams. I'd shifted it to my left hand in order to grasp the bay's mane with the other; the bandage on the bullet-crease in the left had come loose in the meanwhile. I unwound it and threw it away. The wound was still angry red, but it had closed. Taking care to keep it from bleeding again was less of a distraction than the bandage itself.

Distractions I had in plenty. Behind me I heard the pounding of more than one set of hooves. McCready had rallied all the troops handy. Childress had been over-conscientious in writing down his wishes for his campaign against Mexico and the United States to continue after his death. If his captain was this determined to prevent me from reporting back to Washington, he had no intention of abandoning his predecessor's mad dream.

The road narrowed. I slowed my pace, ducking overhanging tree limbs, and took a nearly vertical grade with the reins taut and leaning back parallel with the side of the mountain. The bay picked its way daintily, whistling through its nostrils, eyes rolling over white. That was the test of a good mount; but you never knew how it would measure up until you put your hide on the line. I cursed Judge Blackthorne more often than I praised him, but when it came to outfitting the men he sent into hazard he spent every nickel he kicked and bit the Congress to get, and when it pulled tight its purse strings he chipped in from his own household accounts. This was a good horse.

I found respect then for the creatures who had carried me up that same route by wagon. And I was grateful I'd spent so much of the trip senseless. At times the way was so narrow they had to have rigged ropes to steady the wagons when the outside wheels had no purchase, and just how they'd managed a ton of Gatling has vexed me in all the years since.

The sun was making its rapid descent behind the mountains before I felt secure enough to dismount and lead the bay down the more precarious stretches. After pounding along in the first heat of pursuit, McCready's cavalry had had to slow down, and with darkness piling up the echo of hoofbeats had receded. I didn't dare hope they'd given up, but Childress' insanity hadn't spread so far they'd risk riding that terrain at night. I made a cold camp in the shelter of a shale shelf, sitting up with my back against the Sierras and my revolver in my lap, listening to a healthy set of three-year-old teeth chomping grass and wondering if I'd ever set foot on level ground again.

I dreamed I had, my boots clomping a civilized boardwalk on a street as flat as a lily pond, touching my hat to men and women who'd never heard of Ralph Waldo Emerson and when they spooned sugar into their coffee didn't pause to consider where it had come from and whose bones it had sifted through; and woke in gray light, still a thousand feet above the ocean and Cape Hell.

The birds were awake, singing their sweet melodies of murder. A twig snapped. It was as loud as a pistol report at that empty hour. The birds heard it, too, and went silent. I looked at the bay, standing with its forefeet crossed, eyes shut and breathing evenly; it hadn't stirred in its sleep. I stood and swung the Deane-Adams up the trail, where the danger was greatest. An iron shoe scraped rock. I rolled back the hammer. The crackle echoed among the surrounding peaks, followed by thick silence.

"Do not shoot."

I recognized the voice, the accent. It had been so long since I'd heard it, I couldn't place it at first.

"Come out in the open."

The shoe clanged again, then another and another. I steadied the revolver against my hip, concentrating on the curve of the mountain. Most of a minute passed; I could have measured the time with a calendar. Then a man appeared, leading a gray mule with a rope bridle and only a worn and faded blanket for a saddle.

"It is I, *Senor* Deputy."

I seated the hammer and leathered the pistol. It was the first time Joseph had addressed me as anything more than an equal since he'd promoted himself to engineer.

THIRTY

He wore the white cotton shirt and trousers of Childress' creatures, and sandals in place of his boots. He was pale and gaunt, and when he spoke he broke often to take in air. I took the mule's reins from him, tethered it to a stunted pinon, and helped him into a sitting position under the rock shelf, lowering myself beside him; two pilgrims resting from their travels.

"I didn't think you could make it out of that bed," I said.

"I was awakened by shouting, and guessed the rest. Major Childress—"

"I was there when he died."

"One of those—things was in the room next to mine, with its legs in splints. I took its clothes from a cupboard, and unhitched this animal from a wagon outside."

"How did you get past McCready and the others?"

"I grew up in these mountains. I know a hundred trails to their one."

"You should have stayed where you were. They'd have taken care of you. Without you they can't run the *Ghost*."

"And when they have learned to run it themselves, what? What they did to that man this morning would have been a mercy compared to what would happen if they turned me over to those creatures, as surely they would have done, to keep them *docil*. You saw how I was treated on the way to that devil's place." He flexed his shoulders, still raw from the cross.

"Are you up to this trip?"

"More so than you. You will never find your way to where we were taken following this road. In two miles it winds back into the mountain."

I unfolded the map from my pocket and showed it to him. He shook his head. "This will not get you to Cabo Falso, unless your bones are discovered and brought down the mountain. The Spaniards did not bother to explore this high, with gold so plentiful down below. A man could follow these trails for weeks and finish where he started. Did you forget the man DeBeauclair?"

"He was killed by Childress' men."

"Perhaps. There are creatures as dangerous, men and pumas, and then there are the mountains themselves. Do you think he cared whether he was slain by a bullet or slipped and fell a thousand feet onto his head? Do the men whose bones are piled at Childress' house care? No, *senor*; I did not drag you back from death to see you throw away your life because of a worthless piece of paper."

I put it away and rose. "There's no time to argue."

He ignored the hand I held out and pulled himself to his feet. "I think the captain must give up. Someone must look after the plantation."

"He's got twice as much reason now to keep going."

He did allow me to help him onto the mule's back. He took the lead then. After about a mile we heard hooves ringing on stone. I'd as soon have been proven wrong.

Just about then the grade to our left eased up and we left the road, dismounting to walk our animals through scrub and zigzag washes where the runoff from the rainy season carved treacherous ditches through earth and rock. He kept going as steadily as if he were following a flagstone path, detouring occasionally to go around a dense copse of pine or an enormous boulder, and always returning to his original course—I supposed. For all I made sense of our way we might have been traveling in circles; there were times even when I was sure we were going up instead of down, and I told him so.

"We are," he said, "for the moment. The Mother Mountains are not so kind as the Blessed Virgin."

"Will McCready be taking this route?"

"I think not. There are others easier on horses, but which take them farther out of the way."

I remembered that around noon, when the bay started favoring its left forehoof and with no knife handy I had to use my belt buckle to pry a mesquite thorn from the fetlock. Putting the cavalry farther behind us was a fair trade for the hazards of rough country.

We rested oftener than I liked, despite the advantage. Joseph never complained, but when I saw him list in his seat I reached over to touch his elbow and we dismounted so he could stretch out in the shade and gather strength. He'd started out pale under the brown of his race, and had taken on a yellowish tinge that disturbed me, and his skin glistened with more than just the sweat of effort. But in each case he recovered, or professed to have recovered, in less time than I would have in his condition, and what he knew of the fruits of his native land more than made up for the delay. The roots we ate were edible, however a St. Louis chef might scorn them for their bitter taste and toughness, and he had a botanist's knowledge of which plants flourished in the arid season because of the water they stored in their bulbous roots.

At dark we camped in a horseshoe-shaped depression gouged in passing by the heel of a glacier a million years before Solomon. He scraped the dirt off an albino hunk of twisted vegetation, broke it in two, and handed me half. We crunched and chewed and sat admiring a view New York millionaires shipped themselves first-class to Switzerland to see: thousands of acres of two-hundred-foot pines descending in rows like seats in an opera house to flat white sand—brief as a cuticle seen from that height—and beyond it the empty sky that hung over the blue Pacific.

He tipped back his head and spread his nostrils. They were as wide as shotgun bores. "I smell rain. At the first drop, we climb out of this hole fast as we can manage. I had a cousin who lay down in a dry riverbed to sleep off a bag of wine and woke up drowned to death."

"A puma would have got him sooner or later."

"One did. They are not always partial to live prey."

I laughed like an idiot. The joke wasn't that good, but it seemed I hadn't felt the urge since Helena. He stared at me for most of a minute, then dropped his jaw and let fly with the kind of hooting laughter you never saw in dime-novel Indians. I'd spent enough time with them to know they were gifted clowns, every last one, but it had been so long since I'd been in one's presence when he was in the mood I laughed harder yet, until I choked on my root and he slapped me on my back until I coughed it out.

If a man can love another man without inviting cruel whispers, I loved this one. I never knew what became of him. Three days later, spent crunching through scrub, picking our way across acres of rock, and trotting too briefly along stretches of level road, we came upon the *Ghost,* standing just as we'd left it, with the tree that had blocked it waiting to be removed, as calm as any great beast at rest, and after I traded my stolen gear for my good saddle and bridle from the stock car we parted company. Joseph assured me that my three-hundred-year-old map would get me to Cabo Falso–Cabo Infierno, Cape Hell, whatever you wanted to call it. I'd been there and back without ever seeing the place that sought the honor.

I patted the pocket containing Oscar Childress' last will and testament. It would be evidence enough for the United States to press the Mexican government to lay siege to the late major's plantation; with the usual contingent of U.S. troops serving in an "advisory capacity." That was how we'd taken the Southwestern states from Mexico in the first place.

"In Cabo Falso, where there is law to protect law, you may wire *Los Estados Unidos* and arrange your transportation back to the Montana Territory. Even Captain McCready would not attempt an action there that would place his dead master's grand plan at risk. They haven't everything yet in place; that much I overheard in my sickbed."

"You won't come with me?"

He shook his head. The sallowness was gone from his face, and it seemed to me it had started to take on flesh; although how those blasted roots could contribute to that I couldn't imagine. After forty years I wake from a dream of Mexico with that sharp taste on my tongue.

"I said I wish to be the first of my tribe to drive a train across the length of the Sierra Madre," he said. "What has happened since to make you think I would change my mind?"

"You haven't anything to defend it." I unshipped the Deane-Adams and held it out, butt-first.

One of his rare grins cracked his face, blinding white against the brown. "You will need it more than I, if you are to make your way back to your home. Have we not heard our pursuers, resolute even as of this morning? I have a weapon far more *efectivo*." He slapped the *Ghost*'s cowcatcher. It resonated like a great iron bell. At times I hear it still.